MISSION BRIEFING,

You are Bobby McCloskey, a New York City youth who suddenly finds himself thrust into a world of danger and intrigue. Your new friend, Sam Brock, has been kidnapped by agents of a foreign government after entrusting you with a bag of mysterious green diamonds that seem to hold the secret the agents seek.

What will you do?

You have followed the spies to a moored yacht, where you discover Sam under heavy guard, bound and gagged. Now you must make a choice:

1) You could dump gasoline on the deck and light a fire. In the confusion, you could try to free Sam. Turn to page 144.

2) You could try to lock the guards in the cabin and then find a policeman. Turn to page 135.

3) Or you could search for a way to sabotage the yacht so the spies can't escape. Turn to page 13.

Whichever path you pick, you are sure to find adventure, on your way to becoming the **HERO OF WASHINGTON SQUARE**

HERO of WASHINGTON SQUARE

BY ROSE ESTES

Cover Art by Elmore
Interior Art by Timothy Truman

TSR Hobbies Inc

This book is for the Byrds —
Vicky, Hilton, Quixana,
and Oliver Bearcat. Best friends.

Distributed to the book trade in the United States by Random House,
Inc. and in Canada by Random House of Canada, Ltd.
Distributed in the United Kingdom by TSR (UK), Ltd.
Distributed to the toy and hobby trade by regional distributors.

DUNGEONS & DRAGONS, ENDLESS QUEST, and TOP SECRET are
trademarks owned by TSR Hobbies, Inc.

First printing: May, 1983
Printed in the United States of America.
Library of Congress Catalog Card Number: 82-51207
ISBN: 0-88038-022-5

9 8 7 6 5 4 3 2 1

TSR Hobbies, Inc.   TSR Hobbies (UK), Ltd.
P.O.Box 756   The Mill, Rathmore Road
Lake Geneva, WI 53147   Cambridge CB1 4AD
                                    United Kingdom

id you ever have a problem that you ignored, hoping it would go away, and then it got worse because you ignored it?

That's what happened to me, and that's why I was sitting in the park staring at the *F* on my report card and wondering if there's still a Foreign Legion.

Oh, I won't get spanked or grounded or anything like that. It'll be worse—Dad will say sadly, "I'm disappointed in you, son. I expected better." And Mom will cry.

I'm not dumb. I'm real good in science and math and the other stuff. But English has gotten weird. Diagraming! It ought to be a dirty word! It's almost a foreign language.

Then, we had to memorize and recite a poem! I must be cursed—I got "The Charge of the Light Brigade" by Tennyson. It's fifty-five lines!

I really tried, but every time I got up, my hands started sweating, my throat got dry, and my voice kind of squeaked. Then Miss Rohr would tap her ruler on the desk and say, "Speak up, Robert. We can't hear you."

Sometimes, school is the pits. I'm littler than the other guys and I'm not good at sports, which is all they talk about . . . except for girls.

I don't understand girls at all! When I walk by, they giggle for no reason! Then my face and neck get red, and they giggle more!

Anyhow, there I was in the park, ready to hang myself from the nearest statue, when Pigeon Mary sat down next to me. A bunch of pigeons came with her and for a minute we were buried in birds.

My folks don't approve of Mary, but she and Bagel Ben are my best friends. Ben got his name because his pockets are always full of bagels. He says they're the perfect food—they taste the same fresh or stale and they never spoil. He sweeps out a bakery and gets all the stale bagels he wants for free.

After my folks and the kids at school, Mary and Ben are easy to be around. They don't expect me to be anything special. They like me just because I'm me.

Ben showed up right after Mary, and we sat there feeding the pigeons and eating stale bagels. Then this real old guy wearing a dented cowboy hat, scruffy denim jacket and jeans, and cowboy boots sat down on the bench across from us.

I couldn't help staring—he really looked like a cowboy. But what would a real cowboy be doing in the middle of New York City?

I've heard about not talking to strangers or taking candy till it's coming out of my ears. But somehow . . . this was different.

So I said, "Hi!" and pretty soon he was sitting on our bench, feeding pigeons and eating bagels. After a while, he turned to us and said, "You're the only friendly folks I've met in this city. And although it ain't seemly to burden folks with problems, I'm gonna bust if'n I don't tell somebody soon."

Then he looked all around and said, "I reckon this will sound peculiar, but every word is gospel, or my name ain't Sam Brock.

"I'm a prospector, been one all my life. Never found much, just enough to keep goin'. But last month, Millie—she's my donkey— and me found somethin' real odd. Somethin' that never shoulda been there."

"Gold? Silver? Oil?" I asked.

"Naw! That's normal stuff. I found these." And looking around suspiciously, he pulled a leather thong from around his neck. Dangling at the end of it was a small sack, which he emptied into his hand.

"What are they?" I asked, staring at the tiny green stones. "Don't look like much."

"Like green rock candy," said Mary.

"Like green quartz," said Ben.

"Nope," Sam said, stirring the stones with his finger. "Diamonds."

"Diamonds! Come on, old man! Don't try to kid us," scoffed Mary. "We're New Yorkers."

"Sam, diamonds aren't green," Ben said.

"Are too, if'n they're irradiated," Sam said smugly.

"What's that mean?" Mary asked grimly.

"It means they've been exposed to radiation," I answered.

"Yup," Sam said. "That's pretty smart of you, boy. You must do your homework."

"I like science," I said truthfully.

"Anyhow, that's what this green means. Didn't think much of 'em when I found 'em—just glued 'em on Millie's halter. Never woulda knowed they was special if'n that young oil feller hadn't seen 'em and got all excited. He told me what they were and put me on a plane so's I could get 'em checked out proper.

"Ever since I got here, there've been people yammerin' at me to tell where I found 'em. And they get real mad when I won't.

"Then, this morning I woke up early, and saw these varmints rustlin' my stuff!

"They took every blamed thing except my clothes. They'd have gotten them, too, but I was pressin' 'em under my mattress."

"How did you save the diamonds?" I asked.

"They was in the sack around my neck."

"Did you call the manager or the police?"

"Don't be a durned fool!" snapped Sam. "I'da just been an old man who got hisself robbed. If'n I was robbed at home, I wouldn't call no sheriff. I'd track 'em down myself."

"But, Sam, this isn't the Old West! It's the city. The police protect you!"

"Good point, son. Only thing is, the police was in on it."

"What do you mean?"

"Well, I run after 'em and I found 'em. They was in this alley rippin' my duffel all to pieces. There was three of 'em, and one of 'em was a policeman. I hollered, and the next thing I knowed, instead of runnin', they was chasin' me! I gave 'em the slip, and here I am.

"But now I don't know what to do. I can't go to the hotel and I can't go home—they got my plane ticket and my last dime."

"You have to get help," I said.

"Nope! I need me a hidey-hole, a place to lay low while I figure things out."

"You could stay with me," said Mary.

"Or I'd be proud to have you stay with me," said Ben.

"That's right neighborly," Sam said. "But first I need to hide these here diamonds."

"Give them to Bobby. He's responsible," suggested Ben. "And nobody would think he'd have them."

Sam's eyes stared into mine as if he could see right through me, and then he said, "All right, boy, here!" And he plunked the bag into my hand. "I'm trustin' you. Don't let me down."

I stared at that bag of diamonds and at Mary, Ben, and Sam, all trusting in me, and I wondered what I should do. I knew my parents would not approve of my taking something so valuable, especially if there were danger involved. But how could I refuse to help my friends, who were depending on me?

1) If I ought to help my friends, turn to page 17.

2) If I'm already in enough trouble and shouldn't take the diamonds, turn to page 69.

I lifted Pancho out of his terrarium.

"Ugh. I hate spiders." Mary shuddered.

"Let's hope they do, too," I said as I dragged a chair over to the door. Mary got a baseball bat and stood on the other side. I turned off the light, and we waited. Pancho is almost four inches across and strong for a spider. He was wiggling like crazy. Then the door opened. The big guy poked his head in and I dropped Pancho under his collar.

"Eeeowwll!" screeched the guy as he began jumping up and down. Then, squirming wildly as he ran, he bolted out of the room.

I couldn't help it. I was so nervous, I started laughing, and once I started, I couldn't stop even when Mary pinched me.

But then someone grabbed me by the throat and squeezed—hard. "You like jokes, eh? Laugh at this!" And he poked a gun in my ear.

Then something came swishing through the air, and there was a crunching noise and the man who was holding me collapsed.

"Run!" hollered Mary, grabbing me by the hand. We plowed through the doorway, over a third member of the gang, and stampeded into the kitchen. Mary jerked open the back door and said, "Which way? Where do we go?"

1) "Up to the roof." Turn to page 97.

2) "Down the stairs." Turn to page 145.

The alley was narrow and dark. Buildings on both sides blotted out the sun, making it seem scarier than alleys usually do.

Dumpsters were heaped with garbage. Grease barrels dotted the doorways.

From the smells, I guessed there were lots of restaurants on that block. I was about half-way down the alley. It opened to the street on one end and disappeared around a bend in the other direction.

Soon they'd figure out where I was and be after me again. My side ached and my chest burned. I had to do something that would get me away from them once and for all, so I could get to the police. There were lots of choices, but I couldn't make a mistake this time.

I could:

1) Run to the bend in the alley and hope it led to another street. Turn to page 103.

2) Climb a fire escape and go over the roofs. Turn to page 94.

3) Hide in a dumpster. Turn to page 57.

4) Fight my way out. Turn to page 139.

Moving as quietly as possible, I slipped into the passage. Off to my right was the darkened room where Sam lay. On the left was the room where the guard sat reading. He was sitting sideways to the door. If he chanced to turn his head, he would be looking straight at me.

I thought my heart would stop when the chair scraped along the floor and the guy stood up and started toward the door. Then he smacked his forehead, turned around, and started rummaging through some papers.

I didn't wait until he found what he was looking for but ran down the passage and ducked into the first dark room I came to.

It was the kitchen—I think they call it a galley on a boat. Quietly, I started opening drawers and cabinets, looking for anything that would help. A large, heavy sack dumped over, and a soft dust covered my foot. Sugar!

I grabbed a sharp knife out of a drawer, stuffed it in my pocket, tucked the sack of sugar under my arm, and crept back into the passage. Thank goodness, the guard was still busy, and I was able to sneak out on deck without being seen.

The engine was easy to find. Although I don't know much about engines, I figured that if I cut lots of wires, something wouldn't work like it was supposed to. And for good measure, I poured the entire bag of sugar into the gas tank.

Then I got off the boat as fast as I could. It took ages before I found a telephone, and then

I discovered that I had only enough change left for one call.

1) If I called the police, there was a chance they would think I was a nut. But they might listen. Turn to page 133.

2) I could call a newspaper and hope they believed me. Turn to page 31.

3) I could call my dad and take my chances. Turn to page 104.

The counterman started yelling and everyone ran out front. I crouched behind a stack of packages wrapped in brown paper.

A quick check told me that the clean laundry was the best place to hide. So I snuck up to the basket nearest the back door and climbed in. It was filled with sheets. I probably made a lump, but I burrowed into them and tried my best to lie flat.

Then everyone came back into the room and started looking for me. At least that's what it sounded like. Then the counterman began hollering again.

"Where is he?" growled a deep voice. It had to be Gold Tooth! All the laundry workers started yelling and the gang yelled back. I was scared to death. I figured whoever found me was going to murder me for sure.

Then I heard the back door open, and my basket started to move. From the sound and feel of it, I knew I was being pushed into a truck. Other baskets were loaded, doors slammed, and the truck began to back out.

Then we jerked to a stop and a horn blared. I peeked out and saw a blue van blocking the alley. The driver was one of the gang! Luckily, he didn't see me and I ducked down before he did. After a lot of cursing, the van moved, and we drove away.

My basket was the last stop. Right after I was delivered, someone started lifting sheets. I figured I was safe, so I sat up. Boy, you should have heard that lady scream!

I couldn't think of anything to say, so I just jumped out of the basket and started running. Turned out I had been delivered to a small hotel over on Lexington Avenue, so it didn't take too long to find a policeman. At first he didn't believe me and kept telling me to go away or he'd take me down to headquarters.

"Good, let's go!" I said.

He looked at me kind of funny, but he did it! His captain listened to me and then he called a bunch of other people and they called the FBI and I had to tell the story about ninety-two more times.

Well, they found Gold Tooth and his gang still wandering around where I'd left them and then they found Sam.

Sam says I'm his pal for life and he's going to make me and Mary and Ben all partners in his uranium mine.

Mary was really mad at me for scaring her. She thought I'd been murdered. For a while both she and my mom were hollering at me. Then Dad put his arm around me and said, "Ladies, is this the way to treat a hero?" When they realized what they had been doing, they started laughing.

It's been very interesting. I don't think I'd like to make a career out of it, but this hero business is all right. I wonder if it will work on Miss Rohr?

THE END

I stuffed the bag in my pocket. Then I wrote my name, address, and phone number on a piece of notebook paper and gave it to Sam.

"Don't worry! I'll take good care of them," I said. "Tomorrow's Saturday. I'll be here early, and we'll figure out what to do."

The pigeons were starting to coo sleepily, and I knew I'd better get home. Being late would only make the report card seem worse.

As I got up, I thought I saw someone watching us between the branches of a tree. I started to speak, but then the face vanished so I shrugged it off and said nothing.

Actually, I was anxious to get home and show the diamonds to my dad. I guess I should have told you before this that he's a spy.

Well, not actually a spy. You know James Bond? Well, my dad is like James Bond's boss. He organizes stuff. And he knows everything.

It didn't take long to get home. We live on the top floor of a converted factory. As I unlocked the door, I smelled dinner. It was my favorite—roast beef, corn on the cob, mashed potatoes, and chocolate cake. I decided to let the diamonds wait until after dinner.

"There you are, Robert. Your mother and I were wondering if you'd been kidnapped." My dad chuckled at the old joke.

"Hurry up and wash your hands, dear," said my mom. "Everything's ready."

All through dinner I waited for the right time to tell Dad about Sam and show him the diamonds. But the right moment never came.

Finally, Dad put on his glasses and said, "Well, let's see The Document."

I handed it to him reluctantly.

Using his knife, he slit the envelope and unfolded the paper. After a minute, he put it down and stared at me over his glasses. "Is there some mistake here, Robert?"

"No, sir," I whispered.

"FAILURE, Robert? How could you possibly have failed any subject, much less English?"

I tried to explain about the diagraming, the poem, and the giggling, but it didn't work.

"I'm very disappointed in you, Robert," he said in a tight, quiet voice.

I would have felt better if he'd yelled.

"You realize, of course, that all privileges are withdrawn until this grade is improved. That includes this weekend!"

Until that minute I'd completely forgotten we were supposed to spend the weekend at the shore.

"You will stay at home memorizing this poem and be able to recite it for us, letter perfect, Sunday night when we return."

"Oh, John!" cried my mother.

"Dorothy, you've got to stop coddling the boy. Look where it gets us! I don't ask much, but I do expect a decent report card. Just read these notes. 'Robert is not working up to his full potential and not interacting well with his peers.' No! Being alone for a weekend will give him time to think about mending his ways. No

more discussion—my mind is made up." Then he got up, walked into his den, and shut the door behind him.

I guess Mom tried to change his mind, but it didn't work, because they left first thing in the morning, without me.

"Activate all the alarms," said my father. "Since you won't be going out, you'll be perfectly safe. And remember, I expect to hear that poem when we return."

"Bye, Bobby," said Mom. And as she kissed me on the cheek, she whispered, "You can eat all the ice cream and cake." And then they were gone.

The apartment seemed so big and quiet and empty. I felt abandoned. My hand slipped into my pocket and closed around a leather bag. THE DIAMONDS! I'd forgotten all about them! I'd promised Sam that I would meet him, Mary, and Ben this morning. What would they think if I didn't show up?

But if I did, I'd disobey my father.

1) If I should obey my father, activate the alarms, and start memorizing the poem, turn to page 113.

2) If I should go to the park, tell my friends the problem, and then come home and work on the poem, turn to page 37.

The deli was crowded with people eating lunch. A high glass counter ran the length of the building. Lines of impatient people inched their way forward while men dashed back and forth in back of the counter putting orders together.

Mountains of chopped liver sat on silver trays next to piles of potato knishes. Salamis hung from the ceiling like baseball bats. The sharp smell of open pickle barrels mingled with that of moist, steaming corned beef and pastrami. Great fat links of knackwurst crouched in cocoons of sauerkraut. Rich purple beet borscht bubbled like lava in huge steel vats.

My stomach rumbled as I stood in the line farthest from the door, hoping the gang would miss me.

Unfortunately, they didn't. Parting people like the Red Sea, they plowed into the delicatessen, ignoring the complaints.

I crouched behind a pickle barrel and tried to think what to do.

1) I could attack. Turn to page 79.

2) I could run out the back into the alley. Turn to page 38.

3) I could hide. Turn to page 70.

"I can't believe there are any more of them, Bobby," Mary said. And she reached over, grabbed the doorknob, and opened the door.

"Uh-oh. Wrong choice." There in the doorway, gun gleaming, was another of the gang.

"Thanks for dropping in. It was getting rather boring here," he drawled.

We stood there like dummies, with him pointing his gun at us. Eventually, we were joined by the rest of the gang, who were all pretty angry at us.

We're on some big boat now, down at the docks. Sam's here, but he's all drugged up and can't even talk to us.

They're real uptight now, because they still don't know where the diamonds are. But the boss says they'll find out tonight and then get rid of us.

I think they may have a surprise waiting for them. I'm almost out of these ropes (once a Boy Scout, always a Boy Scout) and being "gotten rid of" doesn't sound too appealing to me. After all, I still have to recite that rotten poem, and I can't do that if I'm dead.

THE END

"Hello, police? My name is Robert McCloskey, and I'd like to report an assault and battery and a breaking and entering."

It took almost an hour, but finally two policemen knocked on the door.

We told them the whole story. Even though they wrote it all down, they kept grinning at each other. When they walked up the stairs afterward, one of them said to the other, "Tell me, Frazetti—how come we always get the fruitcakes?"

"Bobby," Ben said, "I don't think they're going to help. We better do something else."

"Yeah, they thought we were real nuts.

1) "We could go hide out at Mike's." Turn to page 45.

2) "We could go to the park and try to get a policeman there to believe us." Turn to page 88.

Both of us crept out on deck, but the boat kept rising on the waves and then crashing down, making walking difficult.

Then something whined past my head and slammed into the cabin behind me.

"Run, Bobby! It's that feller!" screamed Sam. There was Graf outlined in the light from the cabin, pointing his gun at us.

I raced to the rail, grabbed two life preservers, and shouted, "Jump!"

The water is as cold as ice and the waves are taller than I am. Sam is here next to me. We've lashed the life preservers together with his belt, so we'll stay together.

It's pretty scary, but for the last few minutes we've been seeing a lighted coast. The waves are pushing us in the right direction. With any luck, we'll be there soon.

I sure hope so. The only thing that's keeping me going, other than fear of what might be swimming around my legs, is anger.

We figure that if the police arrest the security guard at the dock, maybe he'll tell them the whole story and they can catch the rest of the gang. And then I can get back to the important things in life, things like grades and poems.

THE END

"I don't like high places and I don't like climbing. But there's only one guy down there and there's three behind us," said Mary. She swung herself over the edge of the roof and started down the fire escape.

Already I could hear footsteps on the stairs. I decided to follow her.

Occasionally, I sit out on the fire escape, but I'd never gone up or down it before. Some of the fastenings looked rusted and loose, and every time we took a step the whole thing would shake and seem like it was going to pull out of the wall. When I looked down I got dizzy. It was just plain awful.

We were passing Mrs. Molinaro's window when I heard a shout and looked up. Goldie and his friends were coming after us!

Mrs. Molinaro and her cats were staring out the window at us. "Help! Call the police!" I yelled. But she didn't even move. One of the cats opened its mouth and made a silent meow. Great! Maybe her window was sound-proof and she couldn't even hear me.

So we kept going, with those creeps right behind, until we reached the end of the fire escape, which is about ten feet above the ground. You stand on a platform, and your weight is supposed to make it lower you the rest of the way. Mary and I jumped on it. It gave a groan but didn't move. Then Goldie yelled at the guy in the alley, who stuck his hand in his pocket and pulled out a gun!

"Come down if you know what's good for

you!" he demanded. By this time he was almost underneath us and the guys above were almost within touching distance.

Mary looked at me and I looked at Mary. "The man says come down. So let's go down," she said with a shrug and, grabbing my hand and clutching her hat, she jumped off, hollering, "Geronimo!"

That poor guy just crumpled under our weight. Lucky for us he was so big, or we might have missed and hurt ourselves. I was picking up his gun when all of a sudden I heard this terrible screech and down came the fire escape with all three guys on it. Well, it stopped with a jerk and BLOOEY! it's raining crooks.

Falling off a fire escape onto concrete isn't fun. At least it didn't look like fun. Goldie fell on his shoulder. I think he broke it. He just lay there moaning. Mary grabbed Goldie's gun and bashed the little guy on the head. The third guy was just trying to sit up when I took his gun, too.

Then it was just a matter of flagging down a police car. They didn't believe me at first, but when I started pulling guns out of my pockets, they followed me fast.

I think the gang was almost glad to see the police. Mary was kind of growling at them and daring them to try something.

Anyhow, everything has turned out OK.

The girls at school have been telling everyone I'm a hero. And everyone seems to agree! I even had my picture taken for the newspaper. The only one who wasn't impressed was Miss Rohr.

"Well, Robert, do you think you can take time out from your heroic schedule to recite your poem for us?"

I was kind of hoping she'd forgotten. But you know what? It wasn't half as bad as I'd imagined it would be. Everyone was looking at me, as usual, but all of a sudden I realized that they were friends, not enemies.

You know, I think I've learned something from this. You can't run away from your problems. If you do, they just get worse. If you take a stand and face up to them, they're usually not half as bad as you imagined. I wonder if that philosophy works when it comes to girls?

THE END

I felt like Daniel stepping into the lion's den as I slipped onto the boat, opened the door to the cabin, and walked in.

There wasn't anyone around, not even the muscleman, so I started searching for Sam.

It wasn't hard to find him. He was lying on a bunk with his hands tied in front of him and a handkerchief stuffed in his mouth.

Like a dummy, I ran straight over to him and started to untie his hands.

"Don't worry. I'm here now. I'll untie you, and everything will be all right!"

Sam gurgled at me, but I went right on. "Don't worry, Sam. It's OK. I've saved you!"

"Oh, but who will save YOU, little wolf cub?" asked a voice with a foreign accent.

I whirled around and there was the muscleman, leaning against the door and pointing a gun at me.

So here we are, Sam and I, all tied up with handkerchiefs stuffed in our mouths.

It's nighttime now and from the roll of the boat, I think we're heading out to sea.

I don't know where we're going or what's going to happen to us. It's pretty obvious that I goofed. I hope there's time for a second chance. Now, let me see, if I can reach these knots with my teeth . . .

THE END

There was a big blue van parked at the edge of the park and we all climbed into it. All the old warnings about not getting into cars with strangers crowded into my mind. How come mothers are always right?

"We'll take the kid down to the dock," said the little guy. "The old man will probably talk once he sees we have him. After we get the diamonds and he signs the claim over to us, we'll decide what to do with them."

The phony policeman was driving and he laughed a nasty laugh.

So here I am in a big mess. Why didn't I listen to my dad? I'd give a year's allowance if I could be at home memorizing that poem.

But I'm not. I'm here. So I better try to figure out a plan to save myself. Maybe Sam will have an idea, but somehow, I'm going to get out of this.

I hope.

THE END

"City Desk, Johnson speaking."

"I wonder if you could help me, please. I have a friend, a prospector, who's been kidnapped. I know it sounds weird, but it's true. At this very moment I'm holding a bag of green diamonds he gave me."

"Yeah. Very interesting. Go crawl back under your mattress, fella."

"No, wait! It's the truth. Do you know what makes diamonds green?"

"They didn't brush their teeth? Here, Mallory, there's a fruitcake on the line. Take it. If there's a story, it's yours."

"Tina Mallory here!" said a young woman's voice.

I don't trust girls, but I didn't have much choice, so I told her everything.

"Where are you now, Bobby?" asked Tina Mallory. I told her. "OK, you stay right there. I'll be there in two seconds!"

Well, it took longer than two seconds, but she was there pretty quick anyway, and she brought two police cars filled with police.

We raced down to the marina and they turned on a spotlight and a loudspeaker and everyone drew out guns. I didn't know if I was scared to death or more excited than I'd ever been in my whole life. Then, the boat began to back away from the dock.

"If they make a break for it, they might make it," said a policeman. "It would take the Coast Guard a while to get here and by then they'd be gone. We'd never find them."

The engine turned over roughly and then caught. My heart sank as I watched the boat disappear into the night.

Then the engine skipped a beat, caught, paused, and then hiccuped into silence. "I did it!" I yelled. "The sugar worked!"

"You did that? You put sugar in their tank? Good boy!" said Tina. Then everyone was rushing around talking to the Coast Guard on radios and calling for more police.

An hour later, the guard was in jail promising to tell tales and name names, and Sam was sitting up, drinking coffee.

"I owe my life to you two. Bobby, you and me are gonna be partners. Fifty-fifty, right down the middle. Right now you're one of the richest kids in New York City. I reckon you can buy that school of yours if you want and fire your teacher. That'll get you out of recitin' that piece."

"Thanks, Sam, but I don't think my mom and dad will let me accept. And after tonight, I don't think anything will scare me again, much less a poem."

I turned to Tina and said, "I'm glad you believed in me. If you hadn't, Sam would still be on the boat."

"Something in your voice told me you were telling the truth, so I took a chance on you, and I'm glad I did. Mr. Brock, Bobby may not be able to accept your offer, but I'll tell you what I want—your story, an exclusive."

"Pretty lady, if'n that's what you want, you

got it. I don't care if Bobby's folks approve or not. He's my partner."

Anyhow, it all ended up OK. Tina wrote a great story and Sam and me had our pictures all over the front page. "HEROIC YOUTH SAVES DIAMOND MINER" said the headline.

My dad even apologized to me! Can you believe that? Even more amazing, Sam took all of us—me, Mom, Dad, Mary, Ben, and Tina—out to eat at a real fancy restaurant with snooty waiters who looked like penguins.

After a few drinks, everyone was talking like they were old friends, and it was great. I don't think there's anything better than having everybody you like liking each other.

Anyhow, no matter how much my folks said no, Sam kept saying yes, so now I own half of a diamond-uranium mine in Nevada. And we're all going out there for our vacation.

So tomorrow I'm going to recite that poem. I won't enjoy it, but I can do it. Watch out, world, here I come! I'm the Hero of Washington Square.

THE END

"Help, Mary!" I yelled. Then lightning shot through my body again, and I sagged to the ground.

I thought I was done for, but as the guy leaned over me, I punched him in the nose as hard as I could. Blood poured down his face, but instead of stopping him, it just made him angrier. He picked me up and threw me over his shoulder, and they all started to run. "Head for the van!" hollered the little guy.

"Help! Help!" I screamed as I bounced and dangled upside down. Lots of people looked at me, but no one tried to help.

"We're coming, Bobby!" shouted Mary. Then a zillion bag ladies started swinging their shopping bags and big, heavy purses.

For a minute I was too surprised to think. But the big guy dropped me and started slugging the bag ladies. That made them really mad.

"Banzai!" hollered Mary, and the fight was on.

Pretty soon there was a big crowd, and everyone was cheering for the bag ladies.

I ran up to the nearest policeman and told him the story, trying to sound as uncrazy as possible.

So here we all are—Pigeon Mary, Two-Bag Sally, Detroit Lil, Brenda from Brooklyn, and a bunch of others whose names I can't remember—sitting in my living room. My folks are being very nice to everyone and trying to understand everything.

My mom asked what she and Dad could do to show their appreciation for rescuing me, and after a lot of hemming and hawing, Detroit Lil asked if we'd let them take a bath.

My folks were surprised, but they never blinked an eye. My mom just said, "Our bathroom door is always open to you."

My dad talked to everyone, and after they all left, he said, "You know, Bobby, I've lived in this city all my life, and I don't think I ever really saw these people before. Some of the careers they've had and the things they've done are amazing. I'm sure my agency could use them in some way. We'll have to talk about it."

THE END

I have to go. I promised them I'd be there. Even if I just explain that I can't stay, it'd be better than not showing up.

But I had to do something with the diamonds. I didn't feel safe carrying them.

I looked around and then thought of just the place to hide them. There's a light hanging outside my bedroom window. It has a misty glow that's real pretty. When I was little, I'd lie in bed pretending that pixies lived inside the light. One day I checked it out—no pixies, but then it was daylight.

Instead, I found a loose brick. I've hidden things behind it ever since. It was the perfect hiding place for the diamonds.

Once I made up my mind, I felt better. It's important to keep your word.

So I locked the door and hurried down to the Square. Only, when I got there, no one was waiting for me.

A twinge of fear nibbled at me as I remembered the face behind the tree.

What if something terrible had happened to Mary and Ben and Sam?

1) If my decision is to go to Mary's home, turn to page 41.

2) If I decide to go to Bagel Ben's basement, turn to page 54.

3) If I decide to go home and wait, turn to page 121.

They were going to find me soon. I looked around hurriedly, but there didn't seem to be anywhere to hide except a pickle barrel, and who wants to hide in a pickle barrel?

So I ducked behind the counter, keeping low, and scurried into the back storage area. A couple of men were there stacking boxes. One of them turned and growled, "Hey, kid, this is private. You can't be back here."

"Oh, I'm sorry. Is there a back door? I'm just passing through."

"Over there. Next time use the front door like everyone else."

"Thanks! I'll do that," I said. Pulling the heavy door open, I stepped into the alley.

1) Right across from the deli's back door was a dumpster filled to the brim with trash. It would be a great place to hide. Turn to page 57.

2) Or I could look around for some other way the alley could be helpful. Turn to page 12.

Acting boldly hadn't done me much good. So I decided to be more cautious—I waited.

The guard and Scouris returned in a few minutes, and Scouris said, "Well, Elmo, it may turn out all right after all. Our friend should be fine until we return this evening. I forgive you for your stupidity. Now help me store the gentleman," and they left again carrying Sam to the cooler.

I took the chance of peeking out and memorizing the license plate of the car. It had diplomatic plates from a country I never heard of—some place called Quarzia.

Then they came back and in a few seconds they were gone, leaving me in the empty warehouse . . . alone with Sam.

I tried not to be too confident. Any number of things could go wrong. They could come back. Maybe I wouldn't be able to find the cooler. Maybe they locked it.

But none of those things happened. I followed their footprints in the dust until I came to the cooler. There were a lot of boxes piled in front of the cooler, but there was no way to lock it.

The hardest thing was trying to wake Sam up. I think he was drugged. Anyhow, I finally did it and even though he was groggy, he was more than willing to get out of there.

We found a loading dock and pried open a side door that led to an alley. After that, it was just a matter of finding a phone and calling the police.

They picked us up and took us to the station, where they listened to our story without interrupting. They took down the number of the car and Mr. Scouris's name and ran it through their computers. Then they called my dad.

I thought he would be mad, but he wasn't.

It seems that our government has been watching the Quarzian diplomats for some time now. They knew they were spying and buying industrial secrets, but they couldn't prove it.

Now, with Sam's and my testimony, they would be able to bring formal charges against them and request that they leave the country.

My dad says I'm a hero. He says that even if I can't memorize my poem, I'm still a winner as far as he's concerned.

You know what? I think I better start memorizing those lines. A little thing like a poem shouldn't bother a hero.

THE END

Mary lives in a statue in a smaller park several blocks from Washington Square. I know that sounds weird, but it's true. Back when the statue was built, they must have planned on using its base to store tools.

What you do is turn one of the statue's hands. Then this concrete slab in the base opens just enough for you to get in. When you're inside, you push a button to get out.

Mary's got it fixed up real nice. There's a water faucet, a cot, a furry rug with hardly any holes, and lots of other stuff. Lit by candles, it's really neat.

I looked around to see if anyone was around. Then I banged on the door.

There was no answer.

"Mary!" I whispered into the vent.

Just then, some people passed by. As soon as they were gone, I twisted the hand of the statue and rushed through the door.

My heart was thumping. It was dark and the room smelled funny. Something was wrong.

"Mary!" I whispered loudly. Just then I stumbled over something lying on the floor.

I rummaged around and found matches and a candle and lit them with shaking fingers.

Mary was lying on the floor. When she saw the light, she struggled to her feet. "I'll get 'em! Let me at 'em!" she cursed.

"Mary, it's just me, Bobby. Sit down and rest and tell me what happened."

Mary flopped on her cot. "My head hurts," she said, touching her head gingerly.

"Oh, Mary, you're bleeding!" Somehow, using lots of cold water and a cloth, we got the bleeding to stop. The cut wasn't half as bad as it had looked. Then I remembered Dad saying that head wounds always bleed a lot.

"Now, tell me what happened."

"Sam and me were eating breakfast, when the door opened and a cop stuck his head in. I figured the police were onto me living here, but then these two goons pushed in.

"Sam had nowhere to run. The cop said, 'Take the old geezer to the Twenty-third Street Marina and stash him on the boat. Then go get the kid and the diamonds. I'll take care of the bird lady.' And then he hit me. The next thing I knew, you were shaking me.

"What have we gotten ourselves into, Bobby? How can we help Sam? We can't just let them take him away like that." Then a look of horror came over her face. "He's got your address! They might get it from him!"

1) If I decide to go after Sam and the bad guys, turn to page 110.

2) If I want to go to my home with Mary and wait for the the bad guys to come after the diamonds, turn to page 67.

3) If I decide to stay with Mary and try to figure out something else, turn to page 115.

"The best defense is a good offense. Let's attack." I grabbed my camera and handed Mary a spray can of furniture polish. "I'll take the door. You take the window."

Then the cans began banging, the bar on the door started sliding out of its groove, and the lock began to turn.

I tried to forget that I was scared. Grabbing the knob, I jerked the door toward me.

Two guys, one big and one little, fell into the apartment. As they scrambled to their feet, I aimed my camera. Bright light exploded in their faces as the flash went off.

"Get him! I'm blinded!" screamed one man.

"I can't see, either!" cried the other. And before they could recover, I turned and ran to help Mary.

Then, WHOMP! I crashed into something big and soft and almost had a heart attack.

"Stand still or I'll shoot!"

"Mary, it's me. Don't shoot!"

"Good. The can's empty. I got him in the eyes and locked the window, but it won't stop him long."

Then there was the tinkle of breaking glass.

"Run!"

"Where?"

1) "My bedroom!" Turn to page 99.

2) "The kitchen!" Turn to page 46.

So here we are at Mike's. We've stayed all weekend, and no one could ever find us. Mike lives in a subbasement under a fancy restaurant. It's safe and warm, and we have lots of leftovers to eat. You'd be surprised what people leave on their plates at these classy places. I suppose I should feel OK, but I don't.

I left my poetry book at home and I won't know that stupid poem. I don't even want to think what my dad will have to say. And we still don't know what happened to Sam.

If I've learned anything from this, I suppose it's that you can't run away from your problems. You may put space between you and them for a little while, but they're still there and will only get worse if you ignore them.

Do you think it's possible to become a bum at thirteen?

THE END

"What can we do in a kitchen? They'll catch us here in two seconds," Mary hissed.

"Trust me, Mary. I've made some deadly weapons here. Even my mom says so. Just you watch!"

Opening the cabinets, I got out some extra-extra-hot sauce and a bottle of peanut oil, poured them into a bowl, and stirred. "This is a lethal brew!" Then I got out a tall jar and filled it with baking soda. I took the cap off the vinegar bottle.

"Now, you take this," I said, handing her a turkey baster and the bowl of hot sauce and oil. "This will start to burn as soon as it hits, so be careful not to get it on you. It may not stop them, but it'll slow them down."

"So what do we do then?"

"That's the back door over there. We can either go up to the roof or down the back steps and hope there's no one waiting for us. Here they come! Get ready!"

I crouched behind the dishwasher, and Mary flattened herself against the refrigerator.

We could hear their breathing as they crept into the darkened kitchen. I was scared they would be able to hear my heart thumping.

When they were about six feet away, I poured the vinegar into the jar, and the stuff started foaming. If you've never seen it happen, trust me. It's real impressive. Anyhow, I tossed it and it landed on them, foaming, bubbling, and hissing.

"Acid! Help!"

It wasn't real acid, of course. It was only vinegar and baking soda. But it stung like acid, so they thought it was dangerous. All except the little man.

"Goldie! Duke! Stop! It's nothing! Get them."

Finally they stopped yelling and moved toward us. My hands felt empty without my potion and that scared me. I reached behind me and felt a wooden pole. The mop! It wasn't much, but it was better than nothing.

Then Mary jumped out and began squirting them with the hot pepper oil. "Take that, you scum! Attack a helpless lady, will you!" I guess she got them in the eyes because they started yelling louder than they had before.

Then she threw the whole bowl on them and they shouted even louder. "Come on, Bobby!" she yelled, and we ran for the door.

In the light of the open door, I saw what we'd done. It was great! They were covered with foam and oil and were rubbing their eyes and howling like crazy men.

"They'll be after us as soon as they wash that stuff out of their eyes. Which way should we go—up or down?"

1) If I decide to go up to the roof, turn to page 97.

2) If I decide to run downstairs, turn to page 145.

"Where do they keep the radio on this critter?"

"Probably in the wheelhouse. But I don't know anything about boat radios."

"That's no problem, boy. I bet I built a dozen crystal radios by the time I was your age. If'n I can find it, I can figger it out. But how do we get around that Graf feller?"

"I could get him to chase me."

"What if he catches you, boy?"

"We'd be no worse off than we are now."

"I reckon you're right. But be careful."

Strangely enough, the door wasn't locked. I guess Graf thought the drug was stronger.

No one was around, so I snuck out onto the deck. I couldn't see very well because there were no lights. A stiff breeze kept whipping a cold, cutting spray of water into my face. It wasn't easy to move, either. The boat kept slamming up and down. I was glad we had decided to stay on board.

Anyhow, I grabbed a railing and hauled myself forward toward the wheelhouse.

There was Graf, all warm and dry, sipping a cup of coffee and looking at a chart.

I stood outside, shivering in the cold, wet wind and got angry. Angry enough to pull open the box on the wall, grab the fire extinguisher, and kick in the cabin door.

Graf looked up in surprise and I pressed the button on the fire extinguisher and got him with a full spray, right in the face.

Thick yellow powder got in his mouth and

covered his head. He started gasping for breath, clutched his throat, and then fell heavily to the floor.

I caught a whiff of the spray. It seemed to suck all the air from my lungs. I backed away from the little cloud that had drifted my way and after a couple of seconds, I was OK. But Graf wasn't. He was making terrible noises, and his face was frozen in a horrible grimace. Maybe I should have left him there, but I just couldn't. I took a deep breath, grabbed his gun, and put it in my pocket. Then I took hold of his heels and pulled.

He was heavy, but I got him as far as the doorway before I had to stop for air.

He lay there in a heap, taking deep, shuddery breaths while I rummaged around in drawers and cabinets looking for rope.

I don't know if the Boy Scouts would give me a badge, but I tied so many knots around his wrists and ankles that he could have died of old age before he wriggled loose.

Anyhow, the rest is history, like they say. Sam found the radio, figured out how to work it, and called for help.

Since neither of us knew anything about boats, we had a hard time telling the Coast Guard where we were. But between us, we figured it out and pretty soon the Coast Guard cutter came alongside and rescued us.

All sorts of people wanted to talk to us—police, FBI, newspapers, magazines, radio, television, and even my dad.

It seems that the diamonds are a poor grade and not really important. But what is important is the fact that when diamonds are exposed to radiation, like from uranium, they turn green.

The guys who kidnapped Sam had hoped to force the exact location out of him and then get him to sign the claim over to them.

Uranium is a rare, incredibly expensive mineral used in nuclear power plants and in making nuclear weapons. Its mining and distribution are carefully controlled by the big governments of the world.

"Well, Robert," said my father, "you've been brave and resourceful and used sound reasoning to get yourself out of a nasty situation. Your mother and I are very proud of you, which isn't to say that we should like you to do this sort of thing often.

"I'd also like to apologize for being so unsympathetic about your problems. On the way to the shore I kept remembering myself at your age. As I recall, I had a few of the same problems. Perhaps we can work on your poem together and I can show you a few tricks I use to remember things. I'll share a secret with you—I still don't like making oral reports myself."

THE END

"I'm not going anywhere with you," I said, and drawing back my elbow, I rammed it into his stomach as hard as I could.

There was a satisfying "Oof!" from the guard, and he doubled over, gagging.

I wrenched loose and ran up the pier and out into the street. When I stopped to look back, he was in his hut, yelling into a phone. I couldn't hear what he was saying, but it wasn't too hard to guess. He was reporting me to a boss.

1) If I stuck around and watched, I would probably find out who was responsible for kidnapping Sam and maybe figure out how to rescue him. Turn to page 119.

2) Or maybe I should just play it safe and call the police. Turn to page 133.

Ben lives in the basement of Kaufmann's Bakery on Bleecker Street, and it took only a few minutes to get there.

I ran down the dark stairs and knocked on the door. At my touch, it swung open.

I walked in slowly. "Ben! You here?"

But other than the soft hiss of the pipes that crisscross the ceiling, there was no answer. I felt for the light cord. Bright light filled the room. Ben was sprawled across his cot, a long smear of blood staining his cheek.

"Ben! Are you all right?"

At first I thought—I hoped—that maybe he had just bumped his head or something. But in my heart I knew he hadn't.

"Let me at them. I'll kill the bums," snarled Ben groggily.

Quickly, I wet a sock—the first thing I found—and patted it all over Ben's face.

"What happened, Ben?"

"I'm not sure myself," Ben groaned as he opened his eyes and struggled to sit up.

"I stayed over at my friend Mike's last night and when I came home, I noticed right off that the place had been dumped."

I looked around the small basement and realized that he was right. Ben isn't very neat, but his room didn't usually look this bad. Clothes hung from pipes, books were strewn across the floor, and stuffing exploded from the shreds of his easy chair.

"I started to go upstairs to ask them what had happened—an explosion maybe—when whammo! someone drops the Empire State Building on my head. When I wake up, this little guy is sitting in my chair and he says, 'That was just to get your attention, Mr. Bagel. My colleagues and I would like you to tell us where the gems are or we shall be forced to jog your memory—jog it rather hard, if you get my meaning.'

"I got his meaning, all right. I understood him fine. He had two big goons standing next to him looking like they'd love to tear me in half.

"So I asked him what he wanted to know. What does he mean, gems? Do I look like a jewelry store? Then he says, 'Very humorous, Mr. Bagel. Tell us where you hid the diamonds and we will leave. If you don't tell us, Kaufmann's Bakery will suffer a most dreadful fire. You, unfortunately, will be a victim of the blaze.'

"What could I do, Bobby? I had to tell them something or they'd of killed me."

My throat got dry and I could hardly get the words past the lump. "Did you tell them I had the diamonds?"

"C'mon, Bobby! What do you take me for? A fink? I'm no dummy. I said they were hidden in the fountain in Washington Square Park.

"Then this guy looks at me and says, 'My friend, I hope you are telling the truth. I should not like to be you if you are lying.'

"Then they slugged me again." Ben groaned. "I need an aspirin. My head is killing me."

"Ben, more than just your head is going to be killing you if we don't get out of here. Remember what they said about lying? I think we ought to get out of here, and real quick!"

"But where could we go? What should we do?"

1) "We could call the police." If this is your choice, turn to page 23.

2) "We could go to the park, find a cop, and point out the bad guys." Turn to page 88.

3) "We could go back to Mike's and hide out." Turn to page 45.

The dumpsters were so full of trash that they would make great places to hide. They'd never find me there! So I hoisted myself up over the edge of the fullest one, slithered down under the bags and boxes, and forced my way into the very center.

I could barely breathe. What air there was smelled horrible. Then I quit worrying about the smell, as I heard someone say, "Check every box, every barrel, every dumpster. Duke, check the other end of the alley. Make sure he didn't get out that way."

Within seconds, Duke returned.

"Blind alley. No way out," he grunted.

"Good. He's still here then. Goldie, block the entrance with the van. We'll search until we find him.

"Come out, kid. You're trapped!" he called.

I didn't answer.

I have to admit I'm getting real nervous. Those creeps are out there tearing the alley apart looking for me, and I hear something chewing, not two feet away from me.

There it is again! It's a gnawing noise. It's coming closer! Now it's sniffing real loud. I can see whiskers. It's a rat!

Cold sweat is running down my sides. The rat is sniffing its way toward me. I hate rats. I'm scared. I don't know what to do. Are heroes allowed to cry?

THE END

"Pick up this end of the clothesline pole and move it over here to the side of the door," Mary said. So I did.

"We'll hide here behind the stairway. When they come out, grab your end of the pole and run around them fast. I'll do the same and maybe it'll work."

There were four lines of laundry on that pole. I don't know why Mrs. Molinaro has so much wash, unless her cats wear clothes. But whatever the reason, I was glad it was there.

As soon as they came out on the roof, all those clothes were waving in their faces, blinding and confusing them.

Mary took her end of the pole and ran around the staircase, howling like a maniac. I took my end and ran the other way.

Those guys never knew what hit them. Oh, they struggled and waved their guns, but the laundry was all over them and they were squashed together and couldn't do much.

I'll never know what we would have done next. You see, we couldn't let go. How do you tie a metal clothespole in a knot? We had to keep a tight hold or they would have gotten loose. We might have been there forever. But then someone started pounding on the inside of the door.

Everyone got real quiet for a minute. Then one of the gang started hollering and Mary and I started yelling, "Help! Police!" at the top of our lungs. Whoever was there ran back down the stairs.

"Who do you think that was?" asked Mary.

"I don't know, but I hope they were on our side, because I don't know how much longer I can hold this pole. My arms are getting tired."

I guess the gang heard me, because they started struggling harder than ever.

Just as I thought I couldn't hold on another second, a deep voice said, "OK, that's it. Hold it right where you are."

Over the edge of the fire escape came two big policemen, with guns drawn.

I didn't care how they got there. I wasn't going to look a gift policeman in the mouth.

It was as good as Christmas seeing those guys all covered with hot oil and laundry, eyes red and puffy, being loaded into a police car.

It took some talking before the police believed our story, but finally they did. They tell us we're heroes. Incidentally, they came because the burglar alarms went off down at the station. I'd forgotten all about them.

There's just one thing I want to know. Do heroes have to recite poems?

THE END

The guard watched me until I passed through the gate, then he walked away. I crouched behind some barrels and started scanning each boat, looking for anything that would tell me where Sam was hidden.

I was studying the sixth boat down when a big, muscular guy came out onto its deck. He looked all around and then nodded to someone below. Another man stepped out on deck. It was a policeman!

The two shook hands and then the policeman stepped off the boat, stopping only to say a few words to the guard and hand over an envelope, which the guard quickly pocketed.

The policeman passed by my barrels and never even saw me. But I saw him. He was big—six-four, 260 pounds maybe—square jaw, mean mouth clamped on a dead cigar. His nose had been broken a few times and his eyes were a flat, cold gray. I was glad he was leaving.

Then the guard wandered off in another direction, and I decided it was time to make my move. The only problem was that I couldn't decide what my move was.

1) Half of me said, Hurry up and get on that boat before the guard gets back. Turn to page 29.

2) The other half of me said, Wait until dark, then get on board. Turn to page 84.

Putting on one last burst of speed, I ran across the street, dodging cars, and into the Chinese-American Village Laundry. Before the counterman could do more than look surprised, I ducked under the wooden counter and ran into the back of the store.

I'd never seen anything like that room. It was like another world. It was one huge room filled with steam—great billowing clouds of it. I couldn't even see the far end! The steam came from big bubbling vats. There were big rolling baskets of unwashed laundry on the left side of the room, and there were bundles of clean laundry being put into more rolling baskets on the right side.

Oriental people, all dressed in white, were busily working. No one paid any attention to me, but I knew they would soon. I had to do something fast.

1) I could hide. Turn to page 15.

2) If the gang found me, I could try to fight. Turn to page 124.

3) Or I could try to find the back door and run into the alley. Turn to page 134.

"Let's just get out of here," Mary said. "I'm too old for tricks or fights. All I want is a cup of hot tea and a nap. Why did I ever get involved in this?"

So I wedged a big barrel in front of the door and we ran over to the outside door. I unlocked it and swung it open and stared at the iron grate that blocked our way. How had I forgotten about that? The basement kept getting broken into so Mr. Scardi had a heavy iron grate built. Only my father and he had keys. We were trapped!

Mary started to cry. Then the lights came on and there they were, with their guns pointed at us.

Wordlessly, we climbed into a van and were joined by a fourth guy who had been left guarding the entrance.

They searched us. Mary hated that and got real mad when they tore her hat apart. She liked that hat. She's muttering under her breath right now and her eyes look mean. It's the same look she had on her face when she mangled the bum who was trapping and eating her pigeons.

I don't know where we're going or what's going to happen. But maybe there's some hope.

I don't know how, but we're going to get out of this. After this, that dumb poem will be a piece of cake.

THE END

". . . and I say to you we must always be aware of the peril of communism," cried the speaker. "Communism surrounds us. Its messengers are everywhere—even here in this crowd—spreading like a virus."

"Yeah, where? I don't see no commies!" jeered a guy who looked like a wrestler.

Another man, clutching a bottle, yelled, "Who you calling a communist? I ain't even voted in ten years! I ain't no communist."

Thinking I was safe, I gulped down my hot dog. But there they were, heading right at me!

"I think yer fulla beans, pal. There ain't no communists here."

"Help!" I hollered. "Give me sanctuary!

"I am Andrei Sergei Gregorovich. My parents escape to USA. Bad mens try to kidnap me so parents will return to Russia. Help, please!" I flung myself at the speaker, and tried to look young, Russian, and helpless.

"I told you we were surrounded by commies," yelled the speaker. "Don't worry, Andy, no one will get you as long as John Quincy Hancock has a breath left in his body!" He picked up a sign that said "Beware Communism!" and waved it around like a bat.

The gang stopped, and the little guy said, "We are not communists. We are relatives. This boy is sick. We're taking him home." He tried to look friendly, but it didn't work.

The big man pulled out a gun and pointed it at the crowd, which began to edge back.

"Put the gun away," cried the little guy.

But it was too late. The crowd went wild. All of a sudden there were shots and then there were cops everywhere.

"That's enough!" yelled a big red-faced policeman. "Let's everyone go down to headquarters and get this straightened out!"

So they loaded all of us in a big police van and drove us down to the station.

Mr. Hancock was confused when I said I was really an American. But finding the gang's guns got the police interested in my story.

They called my dad at the shore and he and my mom left for the city right away. I told them about Sam and where to find the diamonds. Then Mary and Ben found us and told their part of the story.

So here we all are at my place—my mom and dad and Mary and Ben and Sam and John Quincy Hancock. Mom made some hot chocolate and everyone's getting along real good.

Ben and Mary are each carrying on about how the other could have been hurt. I thought you quit that mushy stuff when you got old.

Sam says there aren't any communists in Nevada and invited Mr. Hancock to come visit. Mr. Hancock says he just might do that.

My dad keeps calling me the Hero of Washington Square. Mom just hugs me and says that even heroes have to memorize poems.

THE END

We live on the third floor of what used to be a factory. I started to run up the stairs two at a time, like I usually do, when Mary bellowed, "Hold on, Bobby. I'm not a gazelle." So I went back and took one of her bags, and we walked up together.

On the second floor, Mrs. Molinaro, our weird neighbor, opened her door a crack and peered out at us.

The smell of olive oil, spaghetti sauce, and twenty-seven cats poured out. Ugh!

"Hello, Mrs. Molinaro," I said politely. But she didn't answer, and we kept going.

Four from the top, the stair groaned under our weight and Mary jumped a foot.

"That's our alarm," I joked. "Dad always says he'll fix it, but he never does."

"Be glad he didn't. It's a good alarm." I unlocked the front door and let us in.

"Come on, Mary. They could be here any minute. We've got to get ready. Here, help me with these cans." And the two of us tied empty tin cans together with fishing line and attached the lines to the fire escape window.

"If they try coming in this way, we'll know it. And I've got more ideas."

For the next half hour, the two of us worked feverishly.

While Mary was busy, I went to my bedroom and turned on my computer. I wrote a message telling what was happening and put it on "Quiet Send" with Flash. That means my screen would stay blank, but it would flash repeatedly on the screen of the person receiving it. It's hooked up to the big computer at my dad's office. I just hoped that someone was working on Saturday.

As I finished, I heard the stair groan. And then they were at the door.

"Open up in there! This is the police!"

"Maybe it really is the police," I said.

"And I'm Brooke Shields," said Mary. "Go away. We're not opening this door!"

"We'll get in anyway," hissed a scary voice. "We don't play games with kids and lady bums. Open the door, give us the gems, and we won't hurt you."

"Do you believe them? What should we do?"

"Lady bum? I got my pride. I'm not a lady bum! Let them in! I'm not afraid of them!"

"Mary! Be serious! Look, the way I see it, these are our choices. We can:

1) "Call the police and hope they believe us." Turn to page 150.

2) "Let them in and fight. I've got more ideas." Turn to page 44.

3) "Stall them and hope the alarms and locks work and maybe they'll go away." Turn to page 87.

"I'm sorry, I just can't take them. My folks wouldn't like it."

Mary said, "I'll hide them in my statue. They'll be perfectly safe there."

I stayed as long as I could, but finally I had to leave. I didn't want my folks mad at me for being late as well as for my *F*.

As I left, promising to meet them in the morning, I thought I saw someone lurking behind a tree trunk. But when I looked again, no one was there.

It was as bad as I thought it would be. My dad was very angry and my mom cried. I was grounded for the weekend while my folks went to the shore and I learned my poem.

Now it's Monday and Miss Rohr raised my grade and my dad has calmed down. But something strange has happened—I haven't been able to find Mary, Ben, or Sam anywhere.

My dad says not to worry, that street people move around a lot.

But Ben and Mary aren't like that, and I'm really getting worried. Do you suppose there really was someone behind that tree?

THE END

I guess what I did wasn't smart, but I panicked. They were getting so close, and I couldn't figure out what to do. So I climbed into the emptiest pickle barrel, took a deep breath, and tried to submerge.

Unfortunately, it was still too full, and pickles and juice started pouring over the edge. Even if no one had seen me, the pickles on the floor would have been a dead giveaway. But someone saw me.

"He climbed into the pickle barrel! I don't believe it. Even in New York, I've never seen anyone climb into a full pickle barrel," a lady said as I came up for air.

Then all these people were staring down at me, and one of them was Gold Tooth.

"Please forgive him," he said, acting worried. "He's my cousin and he needs special medication. I'll take him home now."

With one hand he pulled me out of the barrel. With the other he laid two twenty-dollar bills on the counter. "Sorry for the mess. We'll leave now. Come, Robert." And he pulled me along, dripping pickle juice at every step.

"Help! He's not my cousin! He's a kidnapper. He wants to steal my diamonds and murder me. Someone call the police!"

But no one moved. They just stared at me like I was a nut and let him take me away.

I think I am in BIG trouble.

THE END

"Watch closely," I said as I showed her how to work the remote-controlled copters.

"I think I got it. You just press this little thingamajig, then turn this whatsit to make it go where you want. It's simple!"

"No, not simple. We don't have much space. We'll have to be careful to keep them from crashing. Now look at this bag of fireworks I never got to use on July Fourth. If we tie them together like this . . ."

"Gotcha!"

We didn't have long to wait. In the dim light, I saw the doorknob turn slowly. I was under my bed and Mary was under my desk.

"Mary! Your hat! They'll see you!"

"A lady always wears a hat. It stays!"

Then the door opened slowly and the gang filed in. They all had guns.

Shielding my hand, I lit the fuse, hit the copter's start button, and let go.

The roar that little helicopter made was unbelievable! It filled the room, and I swear the walls shook. Then Mary started hers up and you could scarcely hear the guys yelling.

The first firecracker went off. It was so loud my teeth rattled!

The gang was running around the room, crashing into furniture and each other. The helicopters were zooming around their heads and the firecrackers were going off like gunshots. It was great. I loved it, until the big guy saw Mary's hat, snatched it off her head, and poked a gun into her face.

"Get up, lady, and call off the bomb squad or I'll put a hole in your head."

The little guy pulled the curtains, flooding the room with light.

I couldn't risk having Mary get hurt, so I crawled out from under the bed.

"Now, give us the diamonds, and we'll take you to your friend," said the big man.

From the way he smiled, I didn't figure any of us would be coming back.

"I don't think you'll be going anywhere for a while," said a voice from the door.

I don't know who was more surprised, the gang members or Mary and me. We all just stood there with our mouths open.

The big guy, Goldie, pressed his gun against Mary's head.

"Get out of my way. Kidnapping's a federal crime and I'm not going to jail for it. Move, or the lady gets it."

"Where are you going to go? I've got men on the roof, at both exits, and on the fire escape. Give up before you make it worse. Murdering a helpless woman won't help you."

At that, Mary shrieked at the top of her lungs and collapsed like a ton of bricks.

As Goldie stepped backward, trying to get out of the way, I flung myself behind him and he toppled over on top of me.

By the time he got off me, I had about a million questions. "Do you really have all of the exits covered?" I asked as the stranger handcuffed the last of the gang.

"No, I just said that. I'm Davis, Sixth Precinct. The security guard at your father's company called us and said there was a call for help coming from your apartment. When we called here, the operator said there was trouble on the line, so my sergeant sent me over to see what the problem was."

"Boy, am I ever glad you came!" I said as I tried to wake Mary up.

From the sound of Goldie's cursing, I gathered he didn't share my feelings.

"Where's my hat?" said Mary, sitting up and glaring at Goldie. "If you've ruined it, I'm gonna make you real sorry."

Fortunately for Goldie, Mary's hat was all right. Goldie told Officer Davis everything and the police rescued Sam and arrested another guy.

It seems that Sam's diamonds were sitting on top of an enormous vein of uranium. He was going to be rich beyond belief. Somebody in the laboratory where they tested the diamonds was in the pay of a foreign government. They wanted that uranium and would have done most anything to get it. They were going to kidnap Sam, force him to sign the claim over to them, then kill him.

They tell us we're heroes, Mary and me.

I wonder if being a hero will get me out of reciting that poem.

THE END

I turned off the circuit breakers, so there were no lights. The box is in a strange place. If you didn't know where it was, you'd never find it. So it was dark, except for a little light that came through the windows, which no one had washed in a trillion years.

I didn't have a plan till I saw the hose.

Back when the building was still a factory, they used water—lots of it. There was a pipe as big around as a fire hydrant, and a big drainage pit in the floor.

The water had been turned off, the pit covered, and the hose coiled on the wall.

Grunting and straining, Mary and I pulled the cover off the pit. Then I spread an oily tarp over it and piled boxes on its edges until it lay flat, hiding the pit from view.

The hose was stiff and cracked and a couple of pieces flaked off in my hands, but we finally got it hooked up to the pipe.

Turning the water on was harder. The pipe was rusty and stiff with age. Mary and I took turns trying to loosen it.

I could hear the gang getting closer. I was afraid they would find us before we were ready. I was scared to make noise but more afraid of getting killed, so I took a hammer and pounded on the wrench.

Two things happened. The gang figured out where we were and came running. And the pipe gave a rusty shriek and turned.

Water burst into the hose and it jumped in our hands like a wriggling python. A bunch of

little cracks opened and we were soaked to the skin. But the hose held. I shut the water off.

"Take it," I said, handing Mary the hose.

They were very close, so I rushed around the edge of the tarp and waited.

I thought I was going to be sick, I was so scared, but the sight of Mary clutching that hose, hat dangling over her eyes, shook me out of my fear.

Then they were there, not ten feet away.

"Get her! I'll get the kid," said Goldie.

"Leave her alone! I have the diamonds!" I yelled and shook a can filled with tiny nails. It worked. They started toward me.

They were almost at the pit when they stopped.

"It's too easy," said the little guy. "It's a trap. Goldie, shoot the old lady. Show the boy we're serious."

"Banzai!" screamed Mary and hit the hook lever. The rusty hook came rumbling down the track on the ceiling behind the gang. As it picked up speed, it swayed from side to side.

"Shoot!"

"YAHH!" yelled Mary, turning on the water.

I never knew how hard water could be. Even though I was twenty feet away, I was knocked off my feet and drenched to the skin.

Between the swinging iron hook and the water, there was nowhere for those guys to go but into the pit. After the tarp collapsed, they noticed the trap, but it didn't help. Mary hosed them all into the pit.

Just to make sure they didn't get out, I pushed the cover back over the pit and put a bunch of heavy boxes on top of it.

We turned the water off and just stood there, dripping and grinning at each other.

After that, things moved fast. We broke the lock on Mr. Scardi's door and got into his apartment, then called the police.

I didn't tell them the whole story on the phone. I just said that some armed men had broken into our building and a friend and I had trapped them in the basement.

They were there in five minutes.

It took a little while to convince them after they heard the whole story, but the guns did it. The gang couldn't explain why they were in our building armed to the teeth. So they're in jail and Sam has been rescued.

Just as Sam said, his diamonds indicate a rich uranium deposit. Their color proved that. The darker the green, the higher the concentration of uranium. So Sam's rich and I guess Mary, Ben, and I are, too.

Sam says it's to show his appreciation. Without us, he'd have been dead.

The police are still trying to unravel the whole story and find out who was behind it all, but I'll leave that to them. I've had enough adventure to last me a lifetime.

THE END

All of a sudden I got mad. I was tired of these guys chasing me. So they were tough and had guns and wouldn't think twice about killing me. Big DEAL! I was little and fast and, I hoped, smarter than they were.

There didn't seem to be anywhere to hide, and if I ran into the alley, they'd just keep following me. I remembered my dad saying that the best defense was an offense. So I would attack. At least I would have an audience and maybe someone would help me.

Before they could spot me, I ran behind the counter, grabbed a platter of matzo balls, and threw them at the gang. My aim is good and I got every one of them.

"Hey, kid!" screamed a big man by the cash register. "You crazy? Whatsa matter?"

I didn't answer but leaped to the top of the long steam table and sent plates of hot food frisbeeing at the gang!

People started screaming as food flew in all directions. The gang kept grabbing for me, and I tried to avoid them as well as the servers, who were whacking at me with their long serving spoons.

Then one of the servers started to laugh. "Lord, Lord, I ain't seen anything so funny in years." And he stuck his hands in a big silver bowl of chopped chicken liver, molded a big ball, and tossed it into the crowd.

What happened next was great. Even better than I could have imagined.

"Did I ever tell you how much I don't like

you?" growled a waiter to a fat, dumpy lady. "Twenty years I been waiting on you, twenty years I don't like you!" And he picked up her plate and dumped it right over the top of her head.

"Hooray! I always wanted to be in a food fight!" hollered a young guy, and he picked up an enormous apple strudel and threw it!

Lots of people ran out the door as soon as food started flying. Some people, like the man at the cash register, tried to stop it, but I was surprised how many stayed.

Food flew through the air and smeared underfoot. The gang kept trying to get me, but I felt like Peter Pan as I leaped from one spot to the next swinging a giant salami.

Then a bullet whizzed past my ear and thunked into the wall behind me.

"Enough!" hissed Gold Tooth, pointing his gun straight at me. Scraping sauerkraut off his head, he said, "Come down. Now. It's over."

I thought about running, but the little guy wiped his gun off and pointed it at me, too. The third guy looked like he had taken a bath in a pickle barrel. His weapon dripped juice. I wasn't sure if a wet gun would fire. I didn't think so, but I didn't want to test the theory and find out I was wrong.

"Put down the salami and come quietly," Gold Tooth said firmly.

"NOBODY goes NOWHERE!" said the big man behind the cash register, and he clicked the safety off the double-barreled shotgun he was pointing at us. Everybody froze.

"Ever since I was robbed by those gonifs, I keep this gun here. I never had no need for it before. Now, nobody moves until I see the gent that pays for this mess and until it's all cleaned up. You should be ashamed of yourselves, wasting good food like this. There are starving children who could eat for a year on what you wasted. Start cleaning, and you bums toss those guns over here or I'll make holes in all of you."

They didn't like it, but they did it.

I was wiping borscht off the walls when the police came.

The gang tried to run, but Mr. Kaplan put the barrel of the shotgun into Gold Tooth's ear and growled, "Stop!"

I know it won't be easy, but somehow I'll get the police to believe my story. Showing them the diamonds should help. Then, I hope, we can rescue Sam and everything will be all right.

THE END

I passed the time until it got dark by eating. Well, not quite every minute. But I wanted to keep my energy level up, so I ate a few hamburgers, with everything, and some candy bars.

When it got dark, I snuck onto the dock and made my way to the boat.

She was big, maybe sixty feet long. You know, that's something I've always wondered about. Why are boats *she*? Are they ever *he*? What about destroyers? Are they *she's,* too?

Anyhow, I stepped onto the deck and no alarms or whirling lights came on, so I started looking in windows.

There was no one in the wheelhouse, or whatever you call it where they steer the boat. But I found two red containers of gasoline.

The first two cabin windows were dark. The third window was lit. I peeked in carefully and saw the big, muscular man I'd seen earlier. He was sitting at a table, studying some charts and maps. A cup of coffee was sitting on the table. Next to it was a large black gun. There wasn't anyone else in the room, but the door into the passage was open.

I ducked under the porthole and crept away. I made my way around the deck, looking in portholes as I went. On the other side of the boat, in a room directly across from the big guard, I found Sam.

He was lying on a bunk with his hands tied in front of him and a handkerchief stuffed in his mouth.

OK. So I found him. Now what?

I thought about it for a while and then came up with three plans:

1) I could dump some gasoline on the deck and light a fire. While the guard tried to put it out, I could try to free Sam. Turn to page 92.

2) I could try to lock the bad guys in the cabin and then find a policeman. Turn to page 135.

3) I could hide in a cabin and wait until a better opportunity came along. Turn to page 13.

Graf was in the wheelhouse reading maps, so I crept to the lifeboat and got it loose.

It was real windy and the boat was slamming up and down and back and forth. The water looked pretty scary, too, all black and wild with waves taller than me.

"I don't know nothin' about boats, boy. You really think we ought to do this?"

"It's our only chance, Sam. We're getting farther and farther from land. If we stay here, we'll never see another birthday."

"That's a powerful argument, boy. Me and Minnie always did like birthdays."

It was tricky getting the boat into the water with us in it, but we managed. I watched with relief and fear as the yacht disappeared.

"Now what, son?"

"Well, we start rowing, I guess."

"Where's the paddles?"

"They're here. A boat has to have oars."

But there were no oars.

So here we sit in this tiny boat. For a while it seemed like the tide would carry us in to shore. But it didn't.

Now I can't see the shore and I don't even know which direction it is.

I guess we could drift to shore.

I guess we could be rescued. But no one's looking for us.

Except maybe Graf.

THE END

"Bobby, they won't go away. They want those diamonds."

"I know, but these locks are good ones and so are the alarms. They won't be able to get past them." And then, even though I could hardly believe it, the bar on the door moved out of its slot and the tumblers turned in the lock. And if that wasn't enough, the tin cans on the window started to jangle.

"Bobby, they're coming at us from both directions! What do we do now?"

"Run!"

"Run where?"

1) "My bedroom." Turn to page 99.

2) "The kitchen." Turn to page 46.

Mary was sitting on her favorite bench in the park, her largest bag on the ground beside her, stuffed to the brim.

"Mary! Look what they did to me," Ben cried as he collapsed on the bench beside her and pulled off his old felt cap. Already, the bruise had turned an angry purple.

"Ben! Who did this to you?" exclaimed Mary, fussing over him.

"Oh, cut it out, Mary," Ben said, wriggling in embarrassment. "Besides, we gotta get moving, or they'll get away."

"Who? Who are THEY?" asked Mary.

"Let's go somewhere less out in the open," said Ben, "and we'll fill Mary in."

We found an empty concrete chess table in the far corner of the Square and huddled over it. We were surrounded by little old men in berets and beards playing chess, Mah-Jongg, and dominoes. No one even gave us a second glance as we told Mary about the men looking for the diamonds.

Then I added, "Look, the three of us together would be too easy to spot. I think we should separate and come at them from different directions."

"What do we do when we find them?" Ben asked, rubbing his bruised head.

"Find a policeman, point them out, and get them arrested."

"It sounds OK to me. But everyone be careful—no dead heroes," said Mary. "I'll take the left-hand side of the fountain. Ben,

you take the right. Bobby, you take the middle."

I stood and watched Mary and Ben blend with the crowds. Sighing, I pushed my way through a group of street musicians who had set up on the sidewalk. They were attracting a crowd, and I had a hard time getting past them, so I took a roundabout way to the far side of the fountain.

On the way, my stomach started rumbling, so I bought a hot dog from a cart at the edge of the park and piled it with everything—chili, sauerkraut, onions, mustard, and relish. I figured it would hide my face and be a good disguise.

As I pushed through the crowd, I spotted three men in the fountain.

Now, the fountain hasn't worked for a long time. It's big—maybe forty feet across—and has this wide rim around it. Inside there are these steps that lead down to the center. There's no statue in the middle or anything, just a bunch of pipes that used to shoot water into the air when the fountain was working.

The men were crawling around sticking their hands down into the narrow water pipes. I guess they had figured out that nothing was hidden in the fountain because even from where I was standing, I could see the angry expressions on their faces. They were yelling at each other and waving their hands in the air. Then suddenly, in mid-bite of my hot dog, my crowd just melted away, leaving me standing alone.

"It's him!" yelled one of the gang, and they leaped out of the pool and started toward me.

I was scared to death and all I thought of was running. The hot dog still in my mouth, I turned and ran back the way I had come.

1) The musicians were still playing. They had a really big audience now. Maybe I could lose them in the crowd. Turn to page 116.

2) There was a policeman off to my left by some kids playing ball. I could run to him. Turn to page 130.

3) Behind me I could hear a guy lecturing about the evils of communism. People were heckling him, so I knew he had an audience. I could mingle with them and then run away and find Mary and Ben. Turn to page 64.

I found some rags and poured gas on them. The fire started easily. But I guess I used too much gas and, instead of staying in one place, it started spreading and roaring up in big sheets of flame.

I was really scared. All I wanted to do was to create a diversion, not burn down the whole marina.

"Fire! Help! Help!" I cried. Then I ran and hid behind the cabin. Two seconds later, out popped the guard. He saw the fire and ran toward it, cursing.

Before I could lose the little courage I had, I ran into the cabin, down the passage, and into the room where Sam lay tied.

"Sam! I'm here! You're rescued!"

I tried to untie the ropes, but they were tied with knots Boy Scouts never taught me. I pulled the handkerchief out of his mouth and said, "Don't move. I'll be right back."

I ran to the galley, found a sharp knife, and ran back. Overhead, I could hear people running around and yelling.

I sawed through the ropes and said, "Okay, Sam, let's go." Then I looked to see if the corridor was clear.

"It's OK, Sam. Sam?" But Sam wasn't behind me. He was still lying on the bunk breathing heavy and slow.

"Sam! Wake up! You're rescued!"

But he didn't wake up. I guessed from the sweet smell of his breath that he'd been drugged.

I tried to lift him, but he was too heavy, and both of us collapsed on the floor. Then I realized that the noise had died down and flames were no longer reflected on the windows. It was then that I heard him. The guard stood in the doorway, smudged with soot, shaking with anger, and holding a gun.

"Now I have two pigeons in the hand. Nice for me. Not so nice for you."

So here I am, tied up, handkerchief in my mouth, lying in the other bunk, listening to the engines throb. I can tell we've left the harbor and are heading out to sea.

I wonder where we're going. I wonder if I'll ever come back.

THE END

I pulled a barrel over and put it under a fire escape. When I stood up on top of the barrel, I could almost reach the bottom rung of the fire escape.

So I jumped down and found an old broom and then climbed back on the barrel. I stuck the broom through my belt like a sword and then I jumped as high as I could. I missed the first time and almost fell off the barrel. But I made it the second time.

Catching that rusty fire escape was hard, but pulling myself up was awful. How do those guys on TV make it look so easy?

The fire escape kept creaking like it was going to move, but it didn't. I guess it was rusted tight. When I finally pulled myself up, I poked the broom down and tipped the barrel over. It fell with a crash and rolled down the alley. Then I ran up the three rusty flights to the roof.

I got to the top just as the gang, guns drawn, burst into the alley. Then a big blue van drove up and blocked the mouth of the alley.

"Search everywhere. We must find him or Williams will have our ears!" shouted the little man.

Smiling, I thought about the unknown Williams collecting their ears as I ran from one connecting roof to the next.

Two buildings from the end of the block, I stepped into a jungle! There on the rooftop were zillions of flowers, bushes, and small trees growing in big cans and boxes. Even though it was fall, they were still blooming and bearing fruit.

"Nice, huh! I think it's real pretty. It puts me in mind of home."

I almost jumped out of my skin, hearing that voice. I swung around ready to bash with my broom. But it was only this real skinny girl about my age. She had braces on her teeth. Her hair was fiery red and stuck out all over in funny little frizzles. But her eyes were the nicest blue I'd ever seen.

"What are you doing on my roof, anyhow? You got no call to be swinging that mangy ole broom at me on my own roof!"

"I bet you have a zillion freckles," I said, finally noticing the rest of her face.

"You got something to say about pug noses, too?" she grumbled, blushing all the way down her throat.

"I like your nose," I said, still staring at her, "but what happened to your hair?"

"Oh, this! I tried to give myself a home permanent, so I could look like Little Orphan Annie, but I musta done something wrong, because it come out all lookin' like a Brillo Pad, and I look more like Sandy than Annie. But who are you, boy? My mamma don't allow me to talk to strangers. New York City is real dangerous, my mamma says."

"I'm not a stranger. My name is Robert McCloskey and I live only a few blocks away. Your mother is right—strangers can be dangerous. As a matter of fact, some real strangers have been chasing me all over for the last couple of hours, and I climbed up here to get away from them. Do you think I could use your phone and call the police?"

I finally convinced Callie—that's her name, and she's from Georgia—to let me use her phone, and I called my dad at the shore. He listened to me and believed every word.

The police were there in about five minutes. From the safety of the roof, Callie and I watched them arrest Gold Tooth and the others.

They tell me that Gold Tooth and his friends couldn't wait to talk. They kept putting the blame on each other. Anyhow, the police unraveled the whole thing and Sam was rescued by nightfall.

I never thought I'd like a girl, but Callie's different somehow. My mom promised to help her uncurl her hair, and tomorrow night all of us—Callie and her mom and my folks and Ben and Mary and Sam—are going out to celebrate.

My picture is in the paper. They're calling me the Hero of Washington Square.

Callie says I shouldn't let it go to my head—especially a head that can't even memorize a simple poem. But she's promised to help me learn it. Maybe girls aren't so bad after all.

THE END

The door to the roof was open, and Mary and I thundered through it and slammed it behind us. Unfortunately, there wasn't any way to lock it from the outside. I ran to the fire escape and looked down. A big blue van was parked in the alley and a man was leaning against it.

"Well, we can't go down that way. What do we do now."

"All I see is some laundry and clotheslines, a pigeon coop, and those ventilator things," said Mary.

1) "Those are the super's pigeons. He lives in the basement. Maybe he's home. Maybe if we hollered into the vents he'd hear us, and we could tell him to call the police." If this is your choice, turn to page 109.

2) "Sure, and maybe I could pretend I was Wonder Woman and tie them up with the clotheslines." If you decide to try this, turn to page 59.

3) "Or we could climb down the fire escape. Maybe that guy's not part of the gang." If this is your choice, turn to page 25.

"Let's hide, Mary. I know this basement like the back of my hand. They'll never find us."

"Ha!" muttered Mary. But she followed me as I ran into one of the dark halls.

"This is an old coal cellar, from when they still used coal to heat the building. After the last power outage, Mr. Scardi ordered a load of it. 'Just in case we ever need it,' he said. Our furnace can still burn coal. So now, all we have to do is hide under that pile of coal."

"Hide under coal? You've got to be nuts."

"What's better, being dirty or dead?"

"I guess you're right. But I'm not going to like it!"

Have you ever burrowed under a pile of coal? It's not easy. I kept wanting to sneeze.

For a long time we could hear them in the other rooms, cursing and hollering to each other. Then it got real quiet. I haven't heard anything in a while.

I wonder if they're gone? I wonder if it's safe to come out? I wonder if I can peek?

They're not gone.

It wasn't safe.

I shouldn't have peeked.

THE END

"We've got only a couple of minutes at best, Mary. And we've got to come up with a plan that works. If we don't, they'll kill us for sure."

"Well, tell me what to do."

My worktable covers one whole wall and I thought about all the stuff on it. There was my South American tarantula, my model building stuff, a saltwater aquarium, two remote-controlled helicopters, my computer, and some fireworks my folks wouldn't let me set off on the Fourth of July.

The sound of cursing was coming closer.

"Hurry up, Bobby. They'll be here in a second."

"OK, here's what I think.

1) "We can throw Pancho, my tarantula, on them. He'll bite them for sure." Turn to page 11.

2) "We can squirt them with model glue." Turn to page 153.

3) "We can load my remote-controlled helicopters with fireworks and bomb them." Turn to page 72.

Without letting go of my arm, he pulled me forward. After passing six boats, we stepped onto the deck of a sleek, powerful yacht.

Sticking his head into a cabin, he said, "Graf? Got a visitor for you." Yanking me forward, he shoved me through the doorway, and I sprawled on the floor in front of a guy with muscles on top of his muscles.

I stood up and said, "I'm a friend of Sam Brock, and I think he's on this boat. I'd like to see him now!"

"The little sparrow is very brave, no?" said Graf to the watchman.

"I don't like this, Graf. If a kid could find us, the cops could, too."

"Elmo, your mouth, it makes too much noise. Take him away. See that he is quiet."

Before I could do anything, Elmo tucked me under his arm like a doll, covered my mouth with his hand, and then tossed me into a small room lined with bunks. I tried to bite him, but when I opened my mouth, he poured a flood of sticky, sweet stuff down my throat. I gagged, but almost immediately a warm sleepiness spread through me. My brain screamed NO! but my body yawned yes, and I fell asleep.

When I woke up, I felt like someone had stuffed cotton down my throat and poured sand in my brain. I told my body to move, but it ignored me. Finally, I crawled out of the bunk. The floor rolled under my feet and everything was black. It was night and we were at sea.

"How you feelin', boy? Real sorry I got you into this," said a voice—Sam's voice!

"I feel terrible. Where are we?"

"Can't rightly say," said Sam. "But from the way this critter has commenced to rock, I reckon we're on the ocean. How about untyin' me, boy?"

It took me a while, but I finally got the ropes off and Sam stood up and groaned.

"Got any ideas, son? We appear to be in bad trouble."

1) "Maybe we could get to the shortwave radio and call the Coast Guard." Turn to page 49.

2) "We could get two life preservers, jump overboard, and float to shore." Turn to page 24.

3) "We could lower a lifeboat and row to shore." Turn to page 86.

No sooner had I turned the corner of the alley than I heard them behind me.

"There he goes! Hurry!"

I ran as fast as I could, expecting at any moment to see a street crowded with people. What I got was a dead end. Actually, it was a ramp that led down to a big metal door. The handle used to open the door was padlocked to a post in the ground.

Frantically, I looked around for something to protect myself with, or somewhere to hide, but there was nothing.

"HELP!" I yelled at the top of my lungs. But the only answer was the echo of my own voice as it bounced off the brick walls.

Then I heard the sound of a car coming, and I ran toward it in desperation. No matter who it was, I would make him take me with him.

I was yelling and waving my arms as the car turned the corner, but my relief turned to cold fear when I saw a van. It was driven by Gold Tooth! The little man was sitting in the other seat pointing a gun at me.

So here I am, all tied up in the back of the van. I'd like to believe that I'm going to be rescued, or that I could escape, but you know what? I don't think it's going to happen.

THE END

Somehow, I remembered the number of the beach house, asked the operator to call collect, and waited nervously.

"Robert? What's the matter?"

Well, it didn't take much to get me started, and the whole story poured out.

When I finally finished, there was a long silence and then my dad said, "Robert, I believe you. I'm sorry we didn't discuss this before we left. Now, here's what to do. Call this number and say, 'Section Red needs assistance,' and tell them what you've told me. I'll be there as soon as I can.

"And Robert?"

"Yes, Dad?"

"I'm proud of you, son. Be careful."

"Yes, sir. I will, sir." Then he gave me the number and we hung up.

I got the operator again and I did everything Dad said to do.

What happened next was real impressive.

I went down to the marina and waited. Not five minutes later, four black cars pulled up and all these guys got out. You never saw so many guys you wouldn't want to mess around with.

They were dressed for business, with guns and rifles and bulletproof jackets and spotlights and loudspeakers and all kinds of other stuff. The head guy pulled me down next to him behind a storage shed.

"Stay here no matter what happens," he said, and I didn't argue.

They turned on all the spotlights and lit up the sixth boat like a movie marquee.

"Attention, *Gypsy!* You are surrounded! Release your prisoner and surrender!"

I admit it. I was peeking. I saw when the guard slithered out on deck and snaked his way into the wheelhouse. "He's on the bridge!" a man yelled. There was the sound of an engine trying to turn over. It sounded sick. He kept trying, though, right up to when they stormed on board and took him away.

My dad got there after it was all over. By that time, Sam was sitting up drinking coffee and the men were searching the boat.

"High-level technical espionage," the head man said to my dad. "They have enough plans and microfilm on board to start a whole third world technology. I hate to think what would have happened if they'd gotten the old man to sign his claim over to them. From the sound of the diamonds your son described, that deposit is pretty high-grade stuff.

"Incidentally, your boy did quite a job on that engine. Henry Ford himself couldn't have gotten it going."

So now we're going home, all three of us. Dad hasn't said anything yet, but from the way he squeezes my shoulder and looks at me, I know it's OK.

Bet he still makes me learn that crummy poem.

THE END

"Mary, I think I have a plan that will work. Come over here and I'll show you."

"Listen, Bobby, this isn't television. We could get killed. You know what I mean? Real bullets. Really dead!"

"Mary, calm down and listen for a minute. Look here. These cages are where we store stuff that we don't use. Mrs. Molinaro has one and Mr. Scardi, too. They're covered with this chain mesh stuff and no one could break out if they were locked in."

"Easy to say. But how do we get them in there. What do we use for a key?"

"Here's the key. After my bike got stolen from the lobby, my dad made me lock the new one in here at night. Here's what we do. You give me your hat and I tie this fishing line on it and put it in the very back, on top of my hockey stuff. We'll push this furniture down like it fell. Then you start groaning and they'll come running.

"They see your hat—maybe I jiggle it a little. They run in, and I lock the door behind them! Now, doesn't that sound like it would work?"

"It sounds hokey. It would never work."

But it did.

The furniture fell, Mary moaned, and they came running.

As soon as they were all in, I slammed the door behind them and locked it.

When they figured out what had happened, they started pounding on the screen and yelling.

One of them fired a shot that pinged off the furnace.

"What now, Bobby? If we go upstairs, we got a possible guard on the door, a nutty lady who won't let us in, and dead phones in your apartment."

1) "Let's take a chance on there not being a guard on the first floor." Turn to page 22.

2) "We could try to talk to Mrs. Molinaro." Turn to page 151.

3) "Or we could try to get into Mr. Scardi's apartment." Turn to page 122.

"Mr. Scardi, it's me, Robert McCloskey," I shouted. "I'm up on the roof. There are murderers in my apartment! Call the police!"

I kept hollering the same thing over and over, hoping that he would hear me and do something. There was no answer. I don't know if he heard me. I don't even know if he was home. But it sure made a lot of noise. The vent kind of magnified the sound. I should have realized those creeps would hear me, too, but by the time I did, it was too late.

There I was, down on my hands and knees hollering into a ventilator shaft, and there was the enemy standing right behind me with their guns pointed at me.

Mary was at the edge of the roof, calling for someone to help, but no one paid any attention to her.

Well, anyhow, they tied us up with the clothesline and walked us down the stairs.

"Mrs. Molinaro, help! Call the police! I'm being kidnapped!" I hollered as we passed her back door. But there was no response.

The blue van had been moved from the alley and was parked out front. They hustled us into it when they thought no one was looking. But as we drove away, I looked out the back window, and there was Mr. Scardi, writing down the license-plate number.

So keep your fingers crossed. Maybe this isn't . . .

THE END

"Mary, I'm going to try to find Sam."

"And just what will you do if you do find him?"

"Finding him will be the proof we need. Once I find him, I'll call the police."

"Be careful, Bobby. Good friends are hard to come by. I'd hate to lose you."

"I'd hate to be lost. Don't worry. I'll take care of myself." After looking through the vents, I let myself out.

My mom had left me with some money in case of an emergency. So I bought a hot dog and piled it with ketchup, mustard, relish, onions, sauerkraut, and chili and got a can of pop—my breakfast!

There really wasn't a good way to get to the marina by bus or subway, and I thought I'd better not spend my money on a cab, so I started walking. After I finished my hot dog, I was still hungry, so I grabbed another one from a street stand that I passed, just in case I missed lunch. I finished it just before I got to the river.

Those boats are something, all sleek and polished. I'd like to own one someday.

Anyhow, I wandered up and down the marina looking at boats, trying to figure out which one was the right one. I thought I was safe because they'd never seen me. Boy, how wrong can you be!

All of a sudden, someone grabbed my shoulder and squeezed real hard. A raspy voice said, "Lookin' for somethin', fella?"

I looked up into the bloodshot eyes of a snarling security guard.

"Ya got business down here, fella? Or ya plannin' on rippin' somethin' off?"

"I wouldn't steal anything. I was just looking at the boats!"

"No loiterin'!" he snarled. "Them's the rules. If you ain't got no business, yer loiterin', an' that ain't allowed. Beat it!"

Still digging his fingers into my shoulder, he pushed me toward the gates.

When he let me go, I sat down on a curb and thought about what I was going to do. It seemed that I had four choices:

1) Go home. I'd done my best. Maybe they'd come to me since I couldn't find them. Turn to page 121.

2) Go back and talk things over with Mary and try to decide what to do; turn to page 115.

3) Return to the marina openly and see what happens; turn to page 114.

4) Wait until dark and then sneak into the marina to see what I could find; turn to page 84.

I kept hoping, even as I activated the alarms, that Ben or Mary or Sam would knock on the door. But they didn't.

I got my dad's tape recorder and read the poem out loud. Then I played it back. Boy, did I sound funny! When I could finally stand listening to myself, I started trying to recite the poem along with the recording.

Then I discovered if I stared at a spot on the wall and closed my mind to everything, I could recite the poem from start to finish.

By Sunday night I knew it.

By Monday night I had a passing grade.

But I never saw Sam or Mary or Ben again.

I don't know where they went or if they're all right. I hope so.

I still have the diamonds. I've never shown them to anyone. Maybe I will when I'm older.

THE END

I strolled casually down the pier, studying each boat I passed.

I hadn't gotten very far before the guard grabbed me by the arm and snarled, "I thought I told you to get lost."

"I'm sorry, but I can't leave yet. A friend of mine, Sam Brock, is on one of these boats. If I don't find him, I'm going to call my father—he's the police commissioner—and ask him to start a search."

"Sam Brock! Well, why didn't you say so, kid? No problem. I'll take you to him." And he started pulling me down the pier. I didn't know what to do, but I had to decide fast.

1) I could take a chance and go with the guard and hope to find Sam; turn to page 101.

2) Or I could worry about the guard's sudden friendliness and run away; turn to page 53.

Mary and I sat and thought and nibbled on some crackers. Finally I said, "I guess we should go to the police."

"Are you crazy?" groaned Mary. "Sam said a cop helped rob him. For sure it was a cop in here with those creeps. No! No cops. Besides, look at us! Do you think they'd believe us—a kid and a bag lady? I'd lose my home, and your father would be really mad."

Just the thought of my father was enough to stop me in my tracks. So Mary and I just sat there for a couple of hours trying to figure out what to do. Then there was a knock on the door.

"Maybe it's Sam," I said. "Maybe he got away somehow." I leaped up and opened the door and there in front of me, grinning slyly, was a big guy with a gold tooth.

I tried to close the door, but I couldn't. So now we're lying here, Mary and I, tied up like turkeys ready for the oven.

The bad guys—there were two of them—said something about coming back for us after dark. Then one of them laughed and said he hoped we liked ocean trips and swimming.

Somehow, I've got to find a way to get loose before they get back. . . .

THE END

I got away and pushed into the crowd around the musicians. There were six of them—with steel drums, bongos, tambourines, and flutes. They were playing some kind of fast-moving music. Lots of people were dancing and clapping.

Gulping down the last of my hot dog, I dodged in and out and got as close to the players as I could.

The gang came plowing after me, pushing people out of the way. Then people started shoving back. I ducked behind the musicians and watched.

Everyone was mad!

"Get outa my face or I'll reshape your head!" someone screamed, and the big guy with the gold tooth picked him up with one hand and threw him into a steel drum. Then one of the musicians rolled up his sleeves and decked old Gold Tooth!

I decided it was a good time to leave. Once I lost them completely, I could sit down and figure out what to do.

I ran in and out the narrow streets of Greenwich Village, thinking I would be safe there until I could figure out what to do. Then I heard footsteps pounding behind me.

It couldn't be! But it was! Somehow the gang had followed me into the Village!

The little guy had a big bruise down one side of his face and his eye was starting to swell shut. Gold Tooth had blood on his shirt and his nose looked funny. All of them looked like

they were ready to kill me. "Stop that boy! He's a thief!" yelled the little guy.

I started running and they did, too. People watched curiously, but no one tried to stop me. I had to get away ... but how? The street was straight and clear. They were gaining. They'd catch me soon. I had to do something and I had to do it fast.

1) So I ran into Kaplan's Delicatessen. Turn to page 21.

2) So I ran into a Chinese laundry. Turn to page 62.

I did the opposite of what they would expect. Instead of leaving, I stayed. I hid in an old, junky warehouse that was across from the marina. It was creepy, but I had a perfect view of the little guardhouse and the pier. If anything was going to happen, I would be there to see it.

It couldn't have been more than twenty minutes before a fancy car pulled up in front of the pier and a tall dark man with a big hooked nose got out and hurried into the guard's hut.

There was a lot of yelling and arm waving and finger pointing before the two of them left the hut. Big Nose went first and the guard scurried behind, acting like a whipped puppy.

A few minutes later, they reappeared, carrying something heavy wrapped in blankets. They heaved it into the back seat of the car and both of them got in the front seat.

My heart sank. I just knew they were going to drive off and take the bundle, which I was sure was Sam, and disappear forever. But they didn't!

While I was standing there wondering what to do, the car drove straight up to the door of the warehouse where I was hiding. The guard got out and walked toward me. I tried not to panic, telling myself he couldn't know I was there, and I dove for cover.

I crawled into a big cardboard box just as the doors opened and the car drove in.

"This will work well for us. Yes, it will do

until the night falls," said a heavily accented voice . . . Big Nose.

"If the young man does not return with the police by dark, we can return the gentleman to his quarters and carry on as planned. Now, Elmo, what is this establishment? Is there a good place for us to leave our package?"

"It's just an old warehouse, Mr. Scouris. It ain't been used in years," said the guard. "I think there's an old cooler in the back. We could put him in there for a few hours. He couldn't get out."

"Let us look at this cooler. I hope it is better than some of your recent judgments."

"Honest, Mr. Scouris, he used karate on me. I couldn't do nothing. I tried. Honest."

And then they were gone. I could hear their footsteps fading away in the distance. I thought about my options.

1) I could wait until they left and try to rescue Sam. Turn to page 39.

2) Or I could somehow move that car—with Sam in it—out of there. Turn to page 146.

Did you ever think about how many things people want you to do and be? It can get really confusing trying to figure out the right thing. What I mean is—there're things you SHOULD do, things you OUGHT to do, things you WANT to do, and then things you MUST do. It's hard knowing, sometimes.

I had a feeling that no matter what I did this time, somebody was going to be disappointed or angry with me.

I thought about it till my head spun, then I went home and locked all the doors behind me. Mary, Ben, and Sam knew where I lived— they could come get me if they needed me. I just hoped the bad guys didn't know.

I sat down to work on that stupid poem. I kept waiting for the bell to ring, or the phone, but they didn't. I started to go out a million times. But I didn't.

By Sunday night, I knew the poem, and my dad was pleased.

"There now, Robert. That wasn't so painful, was it?"

The fact of the matter is that it *was* painful. I recited my poem and got a passing grade. But I never saw Ben or Sam or Mary ever again. I don't know if they're all right or not. I hope so.

I think about those diamonds and about showing them to my dad. But I never do.

Let the pixies have them.

THE END

"Most people hide a key somewhere around their door in case they lose the one they carry. Let's look around and see if Mr. Scardi hides one, too."

Mary found it. It was hidden under a pile of old clay flowerpots with dirt and dead geraniums in them.

His place was a real dump. It kind of surprised me after the way he fusses at me for tracking dirt into the building. But dirty or no, I didn't care as long as the phone worked. And it did.

It was scary being in someone else's apartment with those guys cursing and hollering threats. But as I dialed the police, I kept telling myself that they couldn't get me.

"Davis speaking, Sixth Precinct."

Keeping my voice calm, I told the story as simply as possible.

"Now, listen, boy, don't you be kidding an old man. Next thing, you'll be asking me if I've got Prince Albert in a can, then telling me to let him out."

"He doesn't believe me," I whispered to Mary. She grabbed the phone away from me.

"You listen to me, Davis, you old bum. This is Pigeon Mary, and every word this boy said is the truth. So you just get a couple carloads of New York's finest over here before those guys get us, or you'll have my death on your conscience."

You know what? They did it! I never thought I'd be so glad to hear a siren.

Anyhow, we got rescued, and Sam did, too. Goldie decided to give state's evidence because kidnapping is a federal offense.

Sam's diamonds aren't too valuable, but the uranium they're sitting on should keep Millie in new bridles for a long time.

Sam gave us each—Mary, me, my parents, Mr. Scardi, Mrs. Molinaro, and Davis—a green diamond and a standing invitation to visit him in Nevada.

The newspapers are calling me "the Hero of Washington Square." Everyone loves me. Everyone except Miss Rohr, who says, "Does this mean you still haven't done your poem?"

I guess you can't win 'em all.

THE END

The back of the laundry looked like the inside of a sauna. There was steam everywhere and it was really hot.

Moving through the murk were all these Oriental people washing and ironing tons of clothes. I guess I could have hidden, but there were so many people in there I was sure to be found.

I was hiding behind one of those big metal racks on wheels that cleaners use to hang finished laundry on, when all of a sudden a bell jangled up front and there was a lot of yelling. Gold Tooth! Then they all burst through the door not ten feet from me.

"There he is!" yelled Gold Tooth, and he whipped out his gun.

The workers all started screaming and running around. I grabbed the rack and shoved it at Gold Tooth. It crashed into all three of the gang and the counterman, too, then turned over, burying them in laundry. I ran through the fog trying not to get caught. I kept thinking that I should have been scared, but I wasn't. It was kind of like playing pinball, only I was the ball.

I rang up some pretty good scores, too, if you can put it that way.

I was just beginning to enjoy myself when Gold Tooth loomed up out of the fog. Before he could grab me, I pushed him into a big vat of hot starch. Then I grabbed a squeeze bottle marked "CLEANING FLUID" and squirted anyone who got near me.

It was getting pretty confusing by this time. No one knew who was who. The workers were really angry. I don't blame them—we just about wrecked that place. They kept hitting us and screaming.

For a while, the gang and I forgot about each other, trying to escape from the angry workers! Then Gold Tooth caught me around the neck and pointed the gun at my head.

The other two pointed their guns at the workers, and suddenly everything got very quiet.

"We're leaving now," said Gold Tooth. "No one stops us, and no one gets hurt."

Then, all the fear I didn't have earlier caught up with me. I was scared to death. I looked down and saw Gold Tooth's arm. It was covered with gobs of gray starch and under the starch his skin was red and puffy. I knew he was badly burned and I knew who was going to pay for it. Me!

We backed out of the laundry slowly. "Help!" I squawked. "Don't let them take me."

But no one moved. After all, it wasn't their fight. We were total strangers who'd practically wrecked their business and then pointed guns at them. Why should they interfere?

We'd reached the front door when a voice said, "That's far enough. Let the boy go, drop the guns, and turn around slowly!"

They didn't, of course. Gold Tooth swung me around, with his gun pressed to my head, and there stood two policemen, guns drawn.

For a minute, it was scary. Then, one of the gang screamed and the other one kind of gurgled. I felt Gold Tooth stiffen and then he let me go. Choking for breath, I dropped to the ground and crawled behind the policemen. Only then did I look back to see what had happened.

It was the workers. They had slipped up behind the gang and twisted laundry twine around their necks! Their faces were dark red by the time the police got the workers to let go.

In a minute a squad car arrived and the gang was handcuffed and taken away. All except Gold Tooth, who had dried into one stiff, hard lump. He was so sore from his burns, I'm not sure he could have sat down, even if he could have bent. They tell me it's lucky the starch was just warming up and not boiling or he'd have been badly burned.

I had Mary and Ben to thank for rescuing me. They had come looking for me, saw what was happening, and almost carried the two policemen to the laundry.

The police also caught the phony cop waiting in a blue van in the alley. He told the police where Sam was and the rest of the story, too.

When Sam had taken his diamonds to the laboratory, they caused lots of excitement. All the technicians knew what the unusual color indicated—uranium, one of the most valuable and sought after minerals on earth. It's used in making nuclear weapons. Unfortunately, one of the technicians was in the employ of a foreign country, a country that would do anything, including kill, for a nuclear capability of its own.

They thought that if they kidnapped Sam they could scare him into signing over his claim to them. Then they would have a legal source of uranium that they could draw upon. They would have killed Sam, of course, and the rest of us, too, if they had been able to. Fortunately, they didn't succeed.

I think everything turned out OK. Sam and Ben and Mary came home with me after the police called my folks.

Things were weird for a while. Everyone was talking and laughing and crying at the same time and I got hiccups.

Sam tried to get Ben and Mary to move to Nevada. But they said that New York is their home, crooks and all.

Now he's talking to my folks, telling them that New York's no place to raise a kid. You know what? My dad is listening! I guess we won't move before Monday, though. I'll still have to do that darned poem. But you know, somehow I don't even mind.

THE END

"They'd leave someone here. So let's go to the basement. Mr. Scardi, the super, lives there. We can call the police."

"OK, Bobby. That makes sense to me," Mary said as she heaved herself to her feet, and we tiptoed down to the basement.

My basement is creepy. When I was a kid I thought monsters lived there. It's got lots of little rooms with thick concrete walls. Some of the rooms extend under the sidewalk. There's a pulley system on the ceiling with a big iron hook attached. I always thought it would be neat to play with, but Dad says it's too dangerous.

"Mr. Scardi," I whispered at his door. But the door was locked. Nobody was home.

"What now, Bobby? I can hear them. They'll be here in a second."

1) "We can go out the basement door and hope no one's outside." Turn to page 63.

2) "We can trick them." Turn to page 107.

3) "We can try to fight them." Turn to page 75.

4) "We can hide." Turn to page 98.

I ran up to the policeman, trying to gulp down my hot dog. I could tell I had smeared it all over my face, so I tried to wipe it off with my fingers. I think I made it worse. But the gang was really close.

I tugged on the policeman's uniform, and he frowned down at me. "You've got mustard on me, boy." He narrowed his blue eyes and glared at me. I opened my mouth, but it was full and all I could do was splutter and point at the gang who were almost upon us.

"It's not polite to talk with your mouth full, boy. Swallow, and then talk."

I tried desperately to swallow that hot dog. But I swear it doubled in size.

With one gulp left, the gang arrived.

I tried to run. The policeman grabbed me.

"Thank goodness you've caught our cousin, officer," said the little man. "His mother is worried sick. He's not quite 'right.' He gets out sometimes and we have to find him."

"Don't believe them! They're kidnappers and maybe even murderers!" I yelled, finally swallowing the cursed hot dog.

"Forgive him, officer. He's really a very nice boy when he takes his medicine. Come along, Robert. Your mamma is worried," and he reached over and grabbed my arm.

"Don't let them take me. They'll kill me. They're just trying to get the diamonds!"

The policeman looked at me oddly. "Such a nice-looking boy," he said as he let go.

I tried to run, but one of the bigger guys

grabbed me by the neck and squeezed. A white sheet of lightning shot through my body. I started to collapse.

"Poor child, he needs his medicine. Thank you, officer. We'll take him home now." Then the big guy scooped me up and walked away.

"Don't try nuthin' else, kid, and you might live a little longer," growled the big guy as he pushed his way through the crowds. He put me down and gave me a little shove, but he kept his hand on my neck. "Try anything funny and you'll be blotto again."

Then I saw Mary. She was standing with some bag ladies, and from the way she moved her hands, I think she was describing me!

I was pretty sure I could get away from the bad guys—I had an idea from a movie I saw once. I could stamp on the big guy's arch. That hurts a whole lot, and maybe he'd let go enough for me to get away.

I knew I had to decide something quick!

1) I could try to get Mary's attention and hope she could do something. Turn to page 35.

2) I could try to get away among the street musicians nearby. Maybe I could lose the gang in the crowd. Turn to page 116.

3) Or I could trust them and hope they'd let me go. Turn to page 30.

"Yeah, sure, kid, and Jack the Ripper is my grandfather," said the policeman who answered the phone.

"Wait! Don't hang up! I'm telling you the truth, really I am."

I guess something in my voice told him it wasn't a joke, because after a minute he said, "OK, kid. Gimme it again from the beginning and don't leave anything out."

I even told him about the poem. Finally he said, "If you're pulling my leg, they'll have my stripes, but stay where you are and I'll send a unit over."

Anyhow, to make a long story short, the boat was there, but Sam and the guard were gone.

The boat was stolen and it was filled with stuff the police were interested in, but there wasn't a clue where they had taken Sam.

I never saw him again. I think about it a lot and often wonder what I should have done differently.

That's really what life is all about, isn't it? Choices. Some good, some bad, and some that just don't work out.

THE END

The counterman must have seen me and followed me into the back of the building.

Boy, that place was horrible. It was all hot and steamy and full of people dressed in white working hard. I didn't see how I could possibly hide or do anything in there, so I headed for the back door.

As soon as those people saw me, they all started yelling. I didn't know what they were saying, but I knew they weren't happy to have me there.

They started pushing and pretty soon I got pushed right through an open door.

It slammed hard behind me and I could hear the lock slide back. I guess they don't like visitors.

I was in the alley.

1) On my left was a dumpster. I could hide in it. Turn to page 57.

2) Or I could look around and see what else I could do in the alley. Turn to page 12.

The passage that led to all the cabins was entered by one door at the rear of the boat. It was solid wood and looked like it could take heavy blows. There was a steel plate on the edge of the door and a matching one on the doorframe that looked like a padlock fit through it.

It was wedged open with a block of wood.

I rummaged around in a small locker and found a long steel bolt and a nut that would screw onto the end of it.

Carefully, quietly, I freed the block of wood and closed the door. Then I slipped the bolt through the bolt hole and screwed the nut on the other end as tight as I could.

I tiptoed off the yacht, ran up the pier, and started looking for a policeman.

But there were no policemen, and the two street phones I found were broken. Finally, I passed a coffee shop. There, sitting at the counter eating his dinner, was a policeman.

"Thank goodness I've found you! I've been looking everywhere," I cried out. And I hate to admit it, but I was near tears.

"What's the matter, boyo? Sara, bring the boy a nice hot cup of tea. Just add it to good old Officer Clancy's tab."

Nothing I said would convince them that a nice cup of tea wouldn't solve my problems.

"Now, then, what's troubling you, boyo?"

I tried to keep it as reasonable as possible, but Clancy was staring at me with sadness in his eyes and shaking his head.

"Officer Clancy, sir. I know how strange it all sounds, but if you'll only come with me, I can prove everything."

It took another five minutes of hard talking, but finally he agreed to come, and we headed for the marina.

"Hurry up. Can't you walk faster?"

"Boyo, I'm due for retirement and I'm walking as fast as these old legs will go. And besides, I'm off duty."

We heard Sam hollering before we could even see the docks.

"Get out of my way, you no-good son of a prairie dog! Stop wavin' that firearm at me. I cut my eye teeth on 'em 'fore you was even borned! Dag-nab it! Let me loose!"

Then there was all kinds of real interesting cursing. I'm trying to remember it all for some special occasion.

Clancy and those old legs of his sped up so fast I could hardly keep up with him. He plowed out onto the pier, pushed through the crowd that had gathered, and jumped onto the boat.

"This is the police! Throw your weapons out and come out with your hands up!"

For a minute there was no answer. Then we heard Sam say, "Better do like he says, sonny, or you'll have to mess with both of us, an' I'm feelin' meaner by the minute."

Then this big black pistol came flying out and landed on the deck and behind it came the muscular guy with his hands on top of his

head. Then Sam popped out, still tied up, but with a big smile on his face.

"Bobby! I kind of reckoned it was you. Come on down here and untie me. I feel like a calf hogtied for brandin'!"

So everything's all right. Officer Clancy called my folks at the shore, and Sam told them the whole story.

My dad was very impressed. Seems that the oil man was right. The only thing that can turn diamonds green is uranium. They have to be real close to it for the process to work. So Sam's diamonds must be sitting on top of a big uranium strike! Dad says he'll put Sam in touch with the right folks and not to worry.

Sam said he wasn't worried, that there was more than enough for him and his partner.

I asked him who his partner was and he just winked and said, "Guess!"

Then he and Clancy went out to tour "some of New York's finer saloons."

As they went down the stairs, Sam was saying, "You know, Clancy, all this city stuff ain't good for a man. You ought to come to Nevada where you can still see the stars."

And Clancy said, "I've been wondering what to do when I retired. . . ."

So all's well that ends well, as someone once said. And I've been thinking that after tonight, memorizing that poem will be a snap.

THE END

I hear some cities don't even have alleys. New York has lots. Some are fairly clean. This alley was terrible. Food scraps flowed out of dumpsters, barrels filled with grease waited collection, and trash crunched underfoot. A tomcat with a torn ear and milky eyes hissed at me. "Don't worry," I whispered. "I'll be gone soon."

It seemed a good place to make my stand. So for the next few minutes I was very busy.

Another noise startled me. It was a dog huddled inside a box. It was a great big dog, with mangy fur and staring yellow eyes. And he was growling at me. Even so, I felt sorry for him as I noticed the bones poking through his skin.

"It's OK, boy," I said softly. At the sound of my voice the fur on the dog's back smoothed down and he quit growling.

I was still petting him when the gang arrived. They didn't see me for a minute. Then the guy with the gold tooth spotted me. Boy, how dumb can you get? They're out for my blood and I'm petting a dog!

"The game's over, you little creep. Let's go," said Gold Tooth. Then he tried to kick the dog aside. But the dog opened its mouth and chomped down on Gold Tooth's ankle!

Gold Tooth screamed and tried to pull the dog off. But the dog hung on. Gold Tooth screamed for his partners to shoot the dog.

Instead, the little man picked up a board and whacked the dog really hard.

The dog let go of Gold Tooth and jumped the little man. Down they went, growling and screaming.

The last guy was trying to get a clear shot at the dog. I ran to this big barrel marked "GREASE" and pushed. It didn't move. Then there was a shot and the dog yelped.

I pushed with all my strength. That did it! A tidal wave of yellow-gray goop cascaded over the guy with the gun.

He tried to grab me. His feet flew up, and down he went in a splash of grease. Before he could get up I dumped another grease barrel.

The stuff oozed and spread over every inch of those guys. The more they struggled, the worse it got. I wasn't taking any chances, so I zipped around to the nearest garbage pail and started throwing whatever I could find—soggy lettuce, overripe tomatoes, empty bottles, and dirty rags.

Just then, there was this loud squeal of tires and a big blue van pulled into the mouth of the alley. The door swung open and out stepped a guy dressed like a policeman. It wasn't fair. I almost had them!

But fair or not, he pointed a gun at me and growled, "Get over here, kid."

I didn't want to go, but what could I do? I walked over to him as slowly as I could.

"Goldie! Duke! Get up! Look at you!"

They really were a mess, all covered with smelly grease and garbage.

Then a voice said, "What's going on here?"

Everyone froze. It was the real policeman from the park! "What's going on?" he repeated.

"Bad timing, buddy," said the phony cop. "Do as I say or I'll shoot our young friend, here. Now, slowly, hand your gun over to me."

I don't know what would have happened if it hadn't been for the dog.

"Look out!" yelled Gold Tooth. But it was too late. We turned just in time to see the dog spring and come flying toward us.

You should have seen it. This enormous dog with about forty trillion sharp teeth, coming straight at us. I mean, it was scary. My heart almost stopped till I realized it wasn't me he was after.

The guy with the gun fired and hit the dog in the shoulder, but it didn't stop him. In about five seconds it was all over.

"That's quite a dog you've got there," the policeman said as he handcuffed the last of the gang.

"He's not my dog, sir. I just met him."

"Well, he's not going to be anybody's dog if we don't get him to a vet soon. Then maybe you can tell me what this is all about."

We found a vet and left the dog there and then went to police headquarters.

The policeman wouldn't put the gang in his car. He said they'd mess it up too much. He made them walk. Before we'd gone a block, Ben and Mary found us. Mary almost squashed me, she hugged me so hard. Then we told the police the story and they believed us!

They called my parents and they came back to the city. At first my dad was mad, but later he even apologized.

My folks looked everywhere except at Mary and Ben. Mom said, "We'd better go, Bobby."

"No!" I said and I grabbed her hands. "Mom, Ben and Mary are my best friends. They care about me and they just risked their lives for me. Don't you think it's time you got to know each other?"

Dad's face got real red like it always does when he gets mad, but then he surprised me. "He's right, Dorothy. We're just a pair of snobs, afraid to look outside our own little world."

So here we all are at my house—me and my folks, Mary, Ben, Sam, and Wolf, my new dog. Sam is staying with us till he goes home.

I asked Dad if there weren't some way we could help Mary and Ben. Dad said that he was working on it and I shouldn't worry.

One friend whose life we've already changed is Wolf. The vet says he's a bull mastiff. Someone did a great job of training him as a guard dog. I don't know how he got abandoned, but I'm sure glad we found each other.

Dad says when his fur grows in and the bandages come off, he'll look just fine. Mom is still scared of him. I think he's great.

THE END

We pounded down those stairs in record time. Mary was huffing and puffing behind me like a runaway train.

We flashed past the second floor and kept going till we skidded to a stop on the first floor. Mary collapsed on the steps.

"I'm not used to this sort of thing, Bobby. I don't know if my heart can take it. I may just die right here," she gasped.

"You can't do that, Mary. It's not safe."

1) "Do we go out this door and run? There might be someone waiting for us." Turn to page 22.

2) "Or do we go down to the basement and try to get away from them down there?" Turn to page 129.

I don't know what made me decide to take the car. I don't know how to drive. I've never even taken Driver's Education. But there was that car, just sitting there with Sam in it. It seemed so easy. After all, how hard can driving a car be? So I crawled out of the box and got into the car. It was just as pretty inside as out, all shiny and new and smelling of leather.

The key was in the ignition. I turned it on. It purred into a soft roar, but it didn't move. I was just beginning to realize that driving might actually be complicated when the guard and Scouris came running toward me.

I panicked. I started moving the lever behind the steering wheel and stomping on pedals, and all of a sudden there was this horrible grinding noise and the car rocketed forward.

The guard and Scouris leaped out of the way as the car rushed past them and plowed into a big stack of boxes.

Scouris was reaching for the door handle, his angry face not two feet away, when I pushed the lever another way and the car hurled itself backward through the wooden warehouse doors, across the street, and into the steel fence of the marina.

The two of them were hollering, "Stop! Stop!" when I moved the lever again, and the car shot away, only this time it went barreling down the wrong side of the street.

I must have mangled every gear in that car and terrorized half the city before the police caught up with me.

"Stop that car!" bellowed a policeman.

At least that's what I think he said. It was kind of hard hearing him over the sirens.

Telling me to stop was a lot easier than my doing it. But I finally realized that if I took my foot off the pedals, it would stop.

You never saw so many police cars. I bet there were twenty of them surrounding me.

"You in the car. Come out with your hands on your head," boomed a bullhorn.

I was so happy that the car had stopped and I hadn't killed myself that I got out of the car grinning happily, until I saw 300 million cops, all pointing their guns at me!

"Hey, it's just a kid!" someone hollered. Then this big policeman grabbed me and said, "Is this your idea of a joke?"

"No, sir, it's no joke." And I started to tell them the story.

"Tell it to the sergeant, kid. Diplomatic plates put you out of my jurisdiction."

Then he climbed into the car, which wasn't so beautiful anymore—I guess I hit a few things while I was trying to get the hang of driving—and drove to the police station.

From then on, it was simple. They let me call my dad and I told him the whole story. He talked to the police and then no one was mad at me anymore!

Sam was still in the back seat, although he had rolled onto the floor during our ride. The police managed to wake him up, and he told his half of the story.

When the Minister of Quarzian Affairs showed up at the police station, raving about the condition of his car, my father was there along with a representative of the State Department.

I don't know what they said to him, but he left soon after, pale and quiet.

When we were driving home, my dad said, "I've been working on this Quarzian matter for over a year. I never expected my own son to break the case for me."

"Are they spies, Dad?"

"Of a sort. Industrial espionage mostly. They've been working up to nuclear armament, stealing everything they could."

"What did they want with Sam?" I asked.

"They didn't want Sam. They wanted his claim. Those green diamonds indicate the presence of uranium. They figured to scare Sam into signing his claim over to them. Then they'd have had a legal supply of uranium. They would have killed Sam and you, too."

Then he thought a minute and added, "Robert, I want you to promise that you won't do things like this anymore. I know you thought it necessary, but your mother and I love you too much to lose you. Promise?"

"I promise," I said.

"Good. Let's go home, then. You and I have a poem to memorize."

THE END

"I'm going to call the real police," I whispered. "Keep talking to them so they think I'm still here." And then I crept away.

"So I'm a bum, am I!" screamed Mary. "It's a good thing you're on that side of the door or I'd reshape your heads. I'm a lady, and don't you forget it."

I picked up the living room phone and dialed O. But when I put it to my ear, there was no sound. I jiggled the button. Nothing. The phone was dead. I ran to the phone in my parents' room and the one on the kitchen wall, and even the separate line in my dad's office, but they were all dead.

"Mary, the phones don't work! They're all dead. I'm scared. What should we do?"

"I don't know, but we better do it fast. They're trying to pick the lock."

Go back to page 68
and make another choice.

We ran back up the stairs and I tapped on Mrs. Molinaro's door. It opened a crack and an eye looked at us over the chain lock.

"Mrs. Molinaro, please let us in. It's important. I have to use your phone."

The door started to close.

"Mrs. Molinaro, if you don't let us in, something terrible will happen to me. And if it does, Dad will never talk to you again."

That worked. My dad is the only one Mrs. Molinaro will talk to. If Mom teases him, he says that Mrs. Molinaro is sad and lonely and we should be nice to her.

Anyhow, she opened the door just enough to let us squeeze through, and then I called the police and told them the story.

"They're coming! I think they believed me!" I said after hanging up the phone.

But Mary and Mrs. Molinaro weren't listening. They were petting the cats.

"This is the mother cat, Mouse, and this is the father, Mickey, and the children are Cleo, Paco, and Wobble. This is Princess—she's from a former marriage. Cats are very fickle," said Mrs. Molinaro.

And Mary petted cats and nodded as though she really cared.

Then the police came and it was real exciting. They caught the three guys and another guy downstairs on the first floor. Boy, I'm glad we didn't go through that door!

I don't understand it all yet. It has to do with industrial spies and espionage.

But I understand enough to know that I'm going to be rich. We all are—Mary, Ben, Sam, and I. It seems that this diamond-uranium mine will make a lot of money, more than Sam says he needs. So he divided it among us because we helped him.

Strange things are happening. It's Mrs. Molinaro. We introduced her to Sam because she helped, too, and POW! It was like lights lit up somewhere. Now it's like a fairy godmother touched Mrs. Molinaro with a magic wand. She almost looks pretty!

Sam said cats shouldn't be locked up in a little apartment, that they need room to run and that Nevada has lots of room. Then he asked her to marry him!

So Mary's going to sublease Mrs. Molinaro's apartment. She and Mr. Scardi are already having big discussions about pigeons. Ben might move into the empty first floor apartment. I'd like that a lot.

So everything worked out pretty good. Even my dad is pleased with my "initiative in dealing with a difficult situation."

Well, almost everything worked out. My mom is pretty mad at me for almost getting killed and for messing up the apartment. One guess who has to clean it up (Mary says she'll help). And I still have to memorize that poem!

THE END

I put a fresh cartridge in my glue gun, plugged it in, and turned it on high. Then I gave Mary two big tubes of model glue. It's not as strong or as toxic as super glue, but it dries fast and holds real good. Then we crouched behind the door and waited.

I could hear them bumbling in the dark, and then the door started to open. A hand reached in and flicked on the light switch, but I had unscrewed the bulb. All three crept into the room.

We let them get all the way inside before we slammed the door and attacked with the glue. I aimed for their heads. I know you're supposed to keep it out of your eyes, but it was water soluble and I bet not too many people use it in self-defense!

Glue was everywhere. I probably used more than I needed, but once I got started, it was hard to stop.

"Take that, you crummy bums!" screamed Mary, and then I guess her glue ran out, because she grabbed the pillows from my bed and started hitting the gang with them. My mom buys only feather pillows, so I'm sure you can figure out what happened next. Feathers everywhere. Feathers plus glue equal a big mess. Anyhow, I grabbed Mary by the hand, dragged her out of the room, and closed the door behind us.

She was really wound up and angry as the dickens. She didn't want to go, but I finally got her out. We pounded down the steps and banged on Mrs. Molinaro's door, yelling, "Help! Help!" at the top of our lungs.

Mrs. Molinaro opened the door a crack, saw us, and tried to close it. But we pushed it open and I gasped, "Please, Mrs. Molinaro. Please let us use the phone. It's an emergency!"

Mrs. Molinaro looked at us with big eyes and gestured silently at the phone. The cats were going back and forth and rubbing all over us as I dialed the police.

I tried to be calm, but it wasn't easy.

"Sixth Precinct, Davis speaking."

"Hello, Officer Davis. My name is Robert McCloskey, and someone just broke into my apartment. There's three of them. They're armed and they tried to kill me. Please come over here right away." Then I gave him my address.

"Are they coming?" asked Mary.

"I think so. Yeah. He sounded like he believed me."

Just then we heard the pounding of feet coming down the stairs.

"Oh, no! They're getting away!"

"I'm not going through this again," said Mary. "Once is enough." Throwing the door open, she stepped out into the hallway.

"OK. Stop right there. One more step and I'll deck you!"

I rushed to the door, and there was Mary, coat sleeves pushed up over her elbows and arms set in a boxer's stance. And I want to tell you, she meant business.

"Shoot her, Duke!"

"I can't. I dropped the gun and my fingers are stuck together!"

"Goldie, do something. She's only an old lady bum. Get her!"

"You get her. I can hardly see through these feathers."

Meanwhile, Mrs. Molinaro's cats had run out the door. They were acting like it was Christmas and their birthday and the Fourth of July all rolled into one.

"Aachhooo! Oh, no! Cats make me sneeze!" moaned the little guy, and he doubled up, sneezing. Cats started crawling on him.

"I'm getting out of here," shouted Goldie, and he put his head down and ran.

Mary just planted herself, pulled back a massive fist, and smacked him in the stomach.

He grunted and started to sag. Mary said, "Watch this, kid. It's my specialty." And she punched him in the jaw with her other fist.

Goldie gave a soft sigh and crumpled on the spot. Right away a cat walked up onto his chest, sniffed him all over, then sat down and started washing itself.

Just then I heard the screech of tires and ran down the stairs as fast as I could.

"Davis, Sixth Precinct. You McCloskey?"

"Yes, sir, and we've got them for you. My friend and I stopped them. They're upstairs."

So that's how it happened.

The police were surprised to find three dangerous industrial spies, which is what they

were. And caught by a bag lady and a kid. But we did it.

It took a while to catch the cats and get them back into the apartment. Then Davis wouldn't put the gang in his patrol car because they were so messy.

"Glue, feathers, and cat fur! Do you have any idea what that would do to my car?"

But he finally did it.

So now here we all are, back in our apartment. Mary has a new hat, Sam's all dressed up, Ben has a new trench coat, and even my dad seems to be having a good time.

Mom's talking to Mary about recipes. It seems Mary used to be housekeeper at a hotel.

I overheard Mom talking to Dad about offering her a job taking care of the apartment.

I hope it happens.

Dad even apologized to me.

"I'm sorry, Robert. If I had been easier to talk to, this never would have happened. I guess I've put too much importance on grades. Your mother and I are proud of you. You showed courage, intelligence, and initiative, which are important grades in themselves."

You know what? After all of this, that poem doesn't bother me anymore. In fact, I know it's going to be simple.

THE END

ENDLESS QUEST™ Books

From the producers of the DUNGEONS & DRAGONS® Game

If you enjoyed this book, look for these additional exciting ENDLESS QUEST™ Books at better bookstores and hobby shops everywhere!

By Rose Estes

#1 DUNGEON OF DREAD

#2 MOUNTAIN OF MIRRORS

#3 PILLARS OF PENTEGARN

#4 RETURN TO BROOKMERE

#5 REVOLT OF THE DWARVES

#6 REVENGE OF THE RAINBOW DRAGONS

#7 HERO OF WASHINGTON SQUARE
based on the TOP SECRET® Game

By Jean Blashfield

#8 VILLAINS OF VOLTURNUS
based on the STAR FRONTIERS™ Game

For a free catalog, write:
TSR Hobbies, Inc.
P.O. Box 756, Dept. EQB
Lake Geneva, WI 53147

TSR Hobbies, Inc